"These guys won't stop till you're dead."

He regretted telling her but there was no denying the facts. Facts he had to keep to himself. The dead woman she'd seen was a DEA agent, and the man in the truck was a cartel member, a cold-blooded killer. Now that Allison could ID him, she had a hit on her.

"I won't let anything happen to you, Allison. I promise."

"Jackson, I'm terrified."

Before he could reply, headlights closed in on them. An oncoming vehicle on their side of the highway. Jackson veered onto a side road and watched the car make a U-turn.

"Get down!"

He floored the accelerator but the vehicle followed them. A gunshot hit the car. Allison screamed.

He had to get her away. But this road led to a dead end—in more ways than one.

"Can you shoot?"

"No." Her eyes widened with fear.

"Tomorrow I'll show you how. For now, you're getting the crash course."

"What if we don't make it till tomorrow?"

Theresa Hall is a native Texan who loves to write suspenseful stories set in small towns with old-fashioned values. She's also a first-grade teacher. When she's not teaching or writing, she likes to read a good suspense book, or binge-watch episodes of *Dateline* or *20/20*. She is a member of RWA's Faith, Hope and Love chapter and ACFW. You can find her online at www.theresalynnhall.com.

Books by Theresa Hall

Love Inspired Suspense

Accidental Target

ACCIDENTAL TARGET

THERESA HALL

LOVE INSPIRED SUSPENSE
INSPIRATIONAL ROMANCE

LOVE INSPIRED® SUSPENSE
INSPIRATIONAL ROMANCE

ISBN-13: 978-1-335-40300-1

Recycling programs
for this product may
not exist in your area.

Accidental Target

This edition published by arrangement with Harlequin Books S.A.

For questions and comments about the quality of this book, please contact us
at CustomerService@Harlequin.com.

Love Inspired
22 Adelaide St. West, 40th Floor
Toronto, Ontario M5H 4E3, Canada
www.Harlequin.com

Printed in U.S.A.

I can do all things through Christ
which strengtheneth me.
    –Philippians 4:13

To my husband for being my biggest fan,
and my family for always believing in me.

ONE

The setting sun cast a purple hue in the November sky. Pellets of sleet stuck to her windshield. "Great. Just what I need."

Allison Moore turned on her wipers and adjusted the defrost. *Dear Lord, please let me get to Maddie's before these roads ice over.* The Texas Hill Country was no place for driving in the winter. Growing up in Houston hadn't given her much experience on these slick, hilly roads.

She hoped Maddie would have a warm fire and a strong pot of coffee waiting for her when she arrived. Her new niece was already two months old and she had yet to hold her. Her oldest niece was participating in a play this Sunday at church, and she'd promised Maddie she would be there. She'd already missed the birth of the baby because of the flu. She wasn't going to be absent for this, too.

A dark shape darted on the side of the road. She held her breath as she tried to think about her next decision. She couldn't slam on the brakes, so she eased her foot from the accelerator to slow down. She remembered what Maddie told her about watching for deer. In their panic, they usually ran into the road without any warning. She slowed down a few more miles per hour hoping to add some brake time if one decided to play chicken with her car. She wouldn't take a chance on anything keeping her from getting to her sister's on time.

She scanned the sides of the highway as she drove. The death grip she kept on the steering wheel was cramping her fingers. She couldn't wait to get off the highway. A sign ahead warned of a sharp curve. She held her breath as she rounded the bend. Headlights blinded her and she squinted to focus on the white stripes to keep from running off the road. But something didn't look right. Headlights illuminated around her.

It was in her lane!

She swerved onto the narrow shoulder. The truck flew past her. She glanced in the rearview mirror to see red taillights spiraling into the air. Allison watched as the lights came to rest sideways against a rocky embankment.

Terror filled her chest as she hit the brakes. Her car spun across the center stripe and stopped in the oncoming lane. Allison pulled the car off the road, flipped on her hazard lights and dialed 911. Her heart pounded in her ears, drowning out the music from the radio. She shut it off and fought to calm her nerves.

The operator picked up.

"There's been an accident on Highway 290 about thirty minutes south of Stonewater! I think we need an ambulance, but I'm not sure." She inhaled several deep breaths to calm herself down.

"Ma'am, can you tell me how many people are involved in the accident?"

"I don't know."

"Are you hurt?"

"No, but I'm sure people in the other vehicle are. I saw it flip in my rearview mirror."

"I'll dispatch an ambulance. Stay there until help arrives. Make sure you're safely off the highway."

"Yes, I am. And thank you."

Allison disconnected the call and drove closer to the accident. With her emergency flashers still on, she got out of her car and shut the door. She activated the flashlight function on her cell phone to light her way as she walked. She glanced up and down the four-lane highway. No cars in sight. She prayed someone would come along soon and be kind enough to stop and help.

Ice crunched under her feet as she approached the black crew-cab truck. A blue tarp lay on the ground about ten feet away. The way it rested against a large rock made it look like something was under it. Maybe it had been ejected from the truck. Whatever it was, it probably wasn't worth anything after hitting against the rocks. She hurried toward the pickup to help the driver. Her foot slipped on a patch of ice and she fell to her knees. A jagged rock tore into her leg. Fresh warm blood seeped into her jeans. Pain screamed through her body as she fought to get back on her feet. The first step caused her legs to buckle. Determined to help whoever was in the truck, she limped on.

Blood tickled her leg as it seeped into her shoes. The cut was bad. A wave of nausea washed over her. She sucked in a deep breath and forced herself to ignore it. Whoever was in the truck might need medical help. Or worse. And she wouldn't be able to forgive herself if she didn't do what she could.

A voice echoed from the cab of the truck. She jerked at the deep raspy sound. She urged her legs to run faster toward the wreckage, but the pain in her knee forced her to lope. She bit her bottom lip with each step. She stopped for a second, reached down and grabbed her knee to steady herself. Wet, sticky blood covered her palm. At least an ambulance was on the way.

She reached the truck and grabbed the side of the overturned bed to steady herself. The broken driver's window littered the ground in jagged bits. Whoever was in there had to be scared and badly hurt.

"Hello? Are you okay? I've called 911. Someone will be here soon. You'll be fine. Just hang in there." The smell of cigarettes filled her nose. Thankfully, she didn't smell any gasoline. She bent down to look inside. Her legs shook from adrenaline and pain. Sounds echoed in her ear as her senses waned. She sucked in a deep breath to steady herself. She needed to prepare her mind for what she might see. The sight of blood always made her faint, and knowing her own was seeping down her leg right now had her on the verge. "Dear God, please give me the strength to do this."

"I'm going to help you out if you can move." Allison peered into the window, and their eyes met and locked. Blood trickled down the man's forehead as he lay tangled in a seat belt. Weeks of discarded fast-food trash covered his body. His face was scarred and pitted. Gray-streaked black hair pulled into a greasy ponytail fanned across his neck. Blood stained his long graying beard. His breath reeked of alcohol, cigarettes and onions. Her stomach rolled as she gagged.

He yelled a few vicious words at her, part English,

part Spanish. Allison backed away and tried to register what he'd said. The light she'd been using flicked off, and she stumbled back into the darkness. She clutched her phone in her hand. Now wasn't the time for her battery to die! She tapped it blindly with her thumb as she fought to focus her eyes on the man inside the truck. Light streamed from her phone into the truck, blinked, then went out again, but not before she noticed the end of a gun pointing at her. A blast resonated inside the truck's cab. Another exploded, then cracked against the rocks behind her.

He was shooting at her!

Fear jolted her body. She erupted into a full sprint toward her car. Pain pulsed in her knee as she stepped on colossal rocks. One misstep and she would be at the mercy of a deranged lunatic. She frantically swiped up with her thumb to find her flashlight function again. Light beamed off the ground and glimmered on something pale poking from the blue tarp. A hand! Terror ripped through her, forcing her to run faster. Was this man a killer? Had he killed the person in the tarp? If he had, she knew he wouldn't stop shooting.

Dear God! Help me, please! I can't die here like this.
Another shot sounded from behind her. She reached her car and fumbled with the door handle. She jumped in and slumped down into the seat. Her breath came in rapid, wheezing gulps. She started the car and slammed it into reverse. The tires slipped on the icy road, making it hard to gain momentum. She glanced over the dash and saw the man crawling out of the truck's back window. He stood and aimed his gun directly at her. She turned off her headlights and punched the accelerator.

Allison spun the car around in the middle of the road. As she drove away in the darkness, she heard a bullet hit the back of the car. He was a good shot, and if she'd left her lights on, she was sure he wouldn't have missed.

She waited until she was far enough out of the range of gunfire, then flipped on her lights. The steering wheel wobbled under her vise grip. Had he shot out her tire?

"Great!" she yelled and slapped the steering wheel. Well, she wasn't stopping. The remaining three tires would have to get her to safety. Between the flat tire and the icy roads, she wasn't sure she'd make it. Her heart pounded in her ears, and she fought back tears. How had this happened? Who was this man?

The steering wheel shuddered harder under her grip. Her tire wouldn't last much longer. She had to pull over. She scanned the road for a place to stop and held her breath hoping she could keep driving a few more miles. The long stretch into town had only a few houses, and most were several yards away from the highway. If only she could drive the next fifteen miles on a flat tire. She knew it was a long shot, but she couldn't make herself stop driving.

Metal scraped the asphalt as the last of the rubber flew from the wheel. Common sense set in, and she accepted the reality that she would have to pull over. She exhaled and stifled the cry lodged in her throat. Without warning, the front of her car spun toward a fence running parallel with the highway. Broken wood and rocks smashed into her windshield. The last thing she saw was the white cloud of the airbag, then her world went dark.

* * *

Sergeant Jackson Archer radioed the dispatcher as he approached a red sedan. "Nine-seven-six requesting information."

"Go ahead, nine-seven-six."

"I thought you said there was a pickup truck involved?"

"That's correct. An overturned truck. Unknown status of the passengers."

Jackson looked around for taillights in the fields surrounding the highway. "All I see is a red car. It's smashed through John Langley's fence. Notify him so his cows don't get out on the road tonight. It won't be long until this highway is impassable with the way this ice is coming down. We don't need it filled with cows."

"We'll let him know."

Jackson parked his police car on the side of the road and climbed out. He approached the vehicle with one hand on his waist resting on his service weapon and the other on his flashlight. He shone it through the driver's window and saw a female with long, light brown hair slumped into the airbag. He opened the door and noticed blood in the car. He felt her neck for a pulse. She moaned as his fingers lightly touched her skin, then bolted up, her brown eyes wide with fear.

"Hello, ma'am. I'm Sergeant Archer. I'm here to help you. Are you all right?" She rubbed her forehead and pulled back her hand to look at it. "You're bleeding a little. It looks like a nasty bump on your head. An ambulance will be here soon to help you."

"I cut my knee."

He peered into the car and aimed his light at her feet.

Blood had soaked her jeans. He swallowed hard and pulled the light away before she could see it.

"I fell."

Tears filled her eyes, and his insides melted. He was sure there was a husband somewhere worried sick about her tonight. "Everything will be fine. I'm going to help you. Can I call your husband for you? Let him know where you are?"

She stared at him for a second before finally responding. "No. I'm not married."

"Any family you can call?"

"My sister. She's expecting me."

She moved to sit up straighter. He laid a hand on her shoulder to still her. Her hair felt like satin on his fingers. "We need the EMTs to check you out before you start moving around. It's only a precaution. Why don't you dial your sister, and I'll let her know where you are."

She pressed the buttons on her cell phone and handed it to him. "Her name is Maddie Porter."

"Maddie Porter is your sister?"

"Yes, you know her?"

"She's my nephew's third-grade teacher this year. He loves her."

"All kids love her," she said, then closed her eyes and leaned back in the seat.

"I'll let her know what happened and that you're being taken to County General for treatment."

He waited for someone to pick up but got a voice mail instead. He left a message and then handed her phone back. "Sorry, she's not answering."

"Thanks. She's probably taking care of the baby or something."

"Can I ask you a few questions about what happened tonight?"

"Sure."

"The 911 operator said there was a pickup truck involved. Can you tell me where that truck is?"

"It's back there," she said, nodding in the direction behind him, then grabbed her forehead and winced.

"Take it easy. That's a big bump."

"No, I'm fine. Just feeling a little nauseous. You have to go back there and check for yourself. Someone was shooting at me. I saw them in my lane. I tried to miss them. I wanted to help, but…" She stopped to catch a breath as if she were having a panic attack.

He put a hand on her shoulder. "Calm down, ma'am. You can't get yourself too upset. It's better if you stay calm."

"But he tried to kill me," she blurted out. Her lip trembled.

He noticed the fear in her eyes. Or was she in shock? She didn't seem to be, but he'd been wrong before. During his ten years in law enforcement, he'd seen a little of everything. "What makes you think he wanted to kill you?"

"Not wanted to. Tried to."

Jackson tried to hide his skepticism.

"He shot at me. Several times. And I… I think he's already killed someone. I think there's a body back there. It's in a blue tarp, lying on the ground against the rocks. I thought I saw a hand sticking out from under it."

Jackson focused on her words. "What makes you think that? Are you sure?"

Her face hardened. "Yes."

He exhaled. If she was right, he'd need every detail. "Let's start over. From the beginning, so I can make sure I get everything."

She closed her eyes, then opened them to stare at him. Her agitation was clear.

"He was in my lane. I swerved. He flipped his truck. I went to help. He shot at me." He didn't flinch at the irritation in her voice. In fact, he didn't blame her.

Red and white lights illuminated the sky as the ambulance pulled in behind his patrol car. He glanced back to see Miles Waverley and a young woman he'd never met before step out of the ambulance. Jackson turned to Allison. "You're in good hands now. Miles will take care of you."

He moved out of the way to allow the paramedics to check her out. He punched the radio on his shoulder and spoke into it. "Nine-seven-six to dispatch."

"Dispatch. Go ahead, nine-seven-six."

"I need backup. I'm still searching for the other vehicle involved. There's a report of an active shooter on the scene."

"Another call came in about ten minutes ago reporting the overturned vehicle. No shooter reported. The person calling it in said they didn't stop to check it out. They only wanted to report it."

"I want to shut the highway down at mile markers seven hundred and six fifty. Go ahead and tell backup I'll meet them there." Jackson turned to the paramedics. "Miles, did you see an overturned pickup on 290 heading over here?"

Miles pulled a neck brace from a backboard. "No, we came here from the station in Stonewater. We didn't see anything from that direction."

Jackson turned to Allison. He didn't want to leave her until he was sure her life wasn't in danger. Right now, he couldn't take that chance. He punched the radio again. "Dispatch, send an officer to wait on me at the ER."

Jackson watched as the medics helped her. "I'm going to follow you to the emergency room. Once I know you're safe, I'll be heading out to the accident to see what we can find. Another officer will stay with you at the hospital until I get back. I'll have more questions for you after you see the doctors."

"I'm sure you will. I just don't know if I'll have the answers you need."

He didn't know if she would, either. Something about her story put him on edge. He doubted someone was a good enough marksman to shoot out her tire in the dark while she was driving away. Could be a fluke, but he wasn't buying it. He walked to the back of her car and ran a finger across the bullet hole in her trunk.

He wasn't sure what to make of her story, but she obviously wasn't lying about someone trying to kill her.

TWO

He wanted to believe her and had no reason not to. But her story seemed odd, even with an obvious bullet hole in her car. He didn't doubt that it had rattled her, but there was something he couldn't put a finger on. He normally had a gut feeling about shady stories. Right now, the hair standing on the back of his neck told him he was stepping into something serious. There was more to this than a scared woman running off the road. He'd left her in the emergency room as soon as an officer had arrived. Now he needed to find out what really happened to her.

Jackson drove up the highway scanning the road to find the overturned truck. His thoughts began to wander as he looked for any signs of an accident. He recalled how Allison Moore looked up at him with fear in her eyes. She didn't seem like a woman making things up. Something bad had happened, and he intended to find out what.

His mind screeched to a halt. There it was. An overturned truck rested against a rocky embankment. Its headlights streaked across the highway.

She wasn't lying. Jackson parked his cruiser on the

side of the road, keeping at a safe distance. Officers should've been here by now. He radioed dispatch again. His training told him to wait for backup. If there was a shooter, he could be anywhere right now. But his gut was telling him that whoever was shooting at her from the truck was nowhere in sight. Within minutes, two Stonewater cruisers pulled up behind him.

Jackson opened his car door and stepped out, careful to keep his eye on the truck. He flipped on his flashlight. Bits of glass cracked under his boots.

"Where have y'all been?"

"We're shorthanded tonight. Weekly and Rappaport went home with the flu. So, what do we have, Archer?"

"It's an odd story. A woman busted through Langley's fence. Her car has a bullet hole in it. She said there was a man in this truck shooting at her. She also thinks there's a dead body in a blue tarp lying on the ground somewhere."

He fanned the light around the truck. Nothing. With caution, he approached. The other two officers went to the opposite side. "Hello?"

No one answered. "I'm Sergeant Archer with the Stonewater Police Department. I'm here to help you."

Jackson bent to shine the light into the cab of the truck. His breath hitched as he stumbled backward. He'd seen more than a few dead bodies during his career, but nothing prepared a cop for the shock of staring one in the face.

He gave himself a few seconds to steady his nerves before looking back into the truck. He swallowed the lump in his throat. Blond hair. His heart seized and he turned away, sucking in a deep breath. Familiar faces flashed before his eyes. He squeezed them shut and did the same thing he always did when this happened. He waited a few seconds until his heartbeat slowed down to a normal pace, then opened his eyes and acted like nothing was wrong.

"Oh, man!" Officer Lance O'Neil, a first-year rookie, threw a fist to his mouth and spun around. It was the first DOA the kid had seen. Jackson didn't admit it out loud, but the years of experience he had on the new cop didn't make it any easier. Staring at death was hard enough, but seeing a body a few days post-mortem was indescribable.

"I wonder who she is?" The rookie peered back into the truck. "Has she been dead for a few days?"

Jackson didn't answer. He scanned the area, then peered back inside the cab of the truck. Something wasn't adding up with Miss Moore's story. It was a fact that someone had shot at her. He'd seen the bullet hole in the back of her car. But who was this woman in the truck? If there'd been a man shooting at Miss Moore, then where was he? Had he killed this woman? He reached up and punched the radio pinned on his shoulder. "Nine-seven-six requesting additional backup at the scene on Highway 290. Send Fredricks with the K-9 unit and notify the coroner. We have a DOA."

Jackson moved away from the truck and waved the other two officers back into their squad cars. "We need to secure the scene. Don't walk around too much or we'll confuse the dog."

He didn't flinch as he leaned against his frozen car door. While waiting for backup, he fanned his flashlight against the ground. A glimmer of something metal caught his eye. The freezing rain had eased up, but a thin coat of ice had already covered the rocks and ground. He grabbed a pen from his pocket and tapped at the shiny circle. It popped loose from the ground, and he realized it was a small silver hoop earring. Maybe it was Allison Moore's. He left it for the detectives to bag as evidence.

He had no clue what to think, but he knew it was going to be a long night. Detective Devon Sparks pulled up in a cruiser. It was a relief to see him so soon.

Jackson and Devon had attended Texas A&M. They'd both pursued degrees in criminal justice. After graduation, they'd attended the police academy together. He loved working with Devon, but they were more than coworkers—they were brothers.

"What've we got here?" Devon asked.

"The victim is a white female, maybe late twenties or early thirties. There's a woman up the highway who says this truck came in her lane and flipped when she swerved to miss it. She's adamant that there was a body in a tarp on the ground. She says it looks like it could've been thrown from the truck when it flipped. And she claims a man inside the truck was shooting at her. She blew a tire out trying to get away and crashed into Langley's fence. She's at the hospital. I left her to check this out. Something isn't adding up with her story."

"No sign of the man anywhere?"

"No, none. I found an earring on the ground over there. You'll need to bag it."

The K-9 unit pulled up, and Les Fredricks opened the door. He held a leash to a large German shepherd named Tito.

"Hey, Fredricks. We're looking for a male, not sure what he was wearing. The only physical description I could get is he has long hair and a beard."

"I'll let the dog check the vehicle, and we'll see what we can find."

"Deceased female is still inside."

"Got it," Fredricks said. He led Tito toward the truck.

Jackson turned to Devon. "Looks like you'll have plenty of help here now. I'm heading to the hospital to question the woman again. I'll meet you back at the station later. Let me know what you find as soon as you can."

"Bring me a pizza on your way back. I was heading home when I got called out."

Jackson gave Devon a pat on the shoulder. "Meet you back at the station. I'm not coming back out here. Pepperoni okay?"

Devon nodded without saying another word. The two of them had an unspoken bond that had grown stronger over the past five years. He didn't have to tell Devon why he wouldn't come back to the scene. It was obvious to Devon and probably everyone else on the force. Ever since he'd lost his wife and daughter, he did his best to stay away from vehicle accidents if he could. Most of the department supported him. The greatest amount of backlash had come from the captain.

Jackson climbed back into his car and exhaled the breath he had been holding. Hope and Natalie had been gone for a long time. Sometimes, it felt like only yesterday. He pulled down his visor and stared at the picture of their faces. Matching blond curls, same blue eyes and sweet smile.

He flipped the visor back up and headed toward town. He was thankful he had this job to keep him busy, but he despised it for making him remember.

* * *

Allison winced as the nurse cleaned her knee. The paramedics had bandaged it, but now it was bleeding again. The gash was too deep to simply cover. To her dismay, the doctor had insisted on stitches. The very thought caused her head to spin and her stomach to flip. She'd always hated hospitals and needles. Now she lay in the emergency room with her hands over her eyes waiting for the inevitable.

"We're about to stitch up her knee. Can you wait a few minutes?"

Relief washed over her. She couldn't wait to see her sister. "Maddie?" She called out from behind her hands, careful not to uncover her eyes for fear of seeing a needle.

"Miss Moore?"

Her heart sank that it wasn't her sister. She moved her hands from her face and squinted as the light hit her eyes. His short brown hair was damp from melted sleet. He raked his hand through it, leaving it messy.

"Miss Moore, do you mind if I talk to you again?"

Allison swallowed and fought to find her voice. His green eyes bore into her.

"Uh, yeah. I guess I can talk." The doctor walked in with his suture tray, and her world began to spin. She covered her eyes with her hands again. "No, no, I'm sorry. We can't talk right now."

"I'm going to numb your skin with a topical, Miss Moore. You shouldn't feel much," the doctor said. His voice lacked any bedside manner to ease her mind.

"Here, give me your hand." The officer reached for her.

Before she knew what was happening, he'd wrapped his large hand around hers.

Gentle. Strong. Protective.

Her eyes flew open.

"Squeeze my hand if you need to." He smiled at her, then winked. "Just not too hard."

"Excuse me, please. I don't mean to interrupt, but I'd like to begin now. If that's okay with you, Miss Moore."

Allison ignored the cranky doctor's tone. She stared into the officer's handsome face and noticed the warmth of his hand around hers. She was more than okay. She felt safe.

"How about I ask you my questions while you get your stitches? It'll take your mind off it."

She could only nod. His eyes sparkled under the lights as he smiled down at her.

"Can you tell me again what you saw out there on the road tonight? Please try to give me all the details, even if you think it's insignificant. It might not be to us."

She nodded. "I was driving and watching out for deer. One almost darted in front of me. Suddenly, there were lights coming at me. I swerved to miss them. When I looked back in my rearview mirror, the truck flipped and landed on its side. I called 911 and went back to check on whoever was in the truck. I saw something on the side of the road as I ran to help. I didn't stop to check it out because I thought someone was injured in the truck. I figured whatever was in the tarp was some cargo from the truck's bed. The weird thing was that when I walked past it, my instincts told me to look closer. I felt like something wasn't right about its shape. I felt it, you know, but I can't explain it."

She took a deep breath and squeezed his hand as the pain seared her knee. "Sorry," she whispered.

"It's going to be all right. I know it hurts." He rubbed the top of her hand with his thumb. "I've had my share of stitches."

The pain in her knee vanished as she focused on his touch. All she felt was the tickle of his skin on the back of her hand. She exhaled the breath she'd been holding.

"When I bent down to look inside the truck, I saw a man. He told me to get out of there…and something else, but I don't want to repeat the nasty words. That's when I heard the gun go off. I didn't even realize what I was hearing at first. It didn't sound very loud, but I know nothing about guns. The first bullet hit the rocks behind me. I heard the crack. He shot again, and I think that's when I realized what was happening. I tried to run back to my car but could hardly make it there. I'd slipped on some ice when I first pulled up. That's how I hurt my knee. I finally got in, turned off the lights and started driving as fast as I could. I think he shot out my tire. I know I'd be dead if he had seen me in the dark. I drove as fast as I could, but my car slid off the road and I wrecked into a fence."

"Can you tell me how you know there was a body in the tarp?"

"Like I told you before, I'm pretty sure I saw a hand sticking out from the blue tarp." She waited for his reaction.

He hesitated. "Was it attached or lying on the ground?"

Her stomach lurched, and she stared at him for a few seconds. "What on earth did you find out there?"

"Sorry, I need you to be specific. We have detectives on the scene, and they might have more questions for you soon." He pulled his hand from hers and wrote something down in his notepad.

"Honestly, I assume it was attached. I didn't stop to pull the tarp back."

"Thank you for cooperating. I know this has been a terrible night for you," he said.

He didn't know the half of it. She focused on the way his eyebrows furrowed as he scribbled in his notepad. She'd almost forgotten all about the doctor stitching up her knee.

"All done. We'll get you up to a private room as soon as one is open," the doctor said.

"Room? Oh, no. There's a mistake here. I'm going home. I'm fine."

The doctor shook his head. "No, you have a concussion. You need to stay overnight. It's not clear yet how you'll be in twenty-four hours. If you have no further symptoms, we'll release you tomorrow."

She covered her face with her hands. "What a horrible night this has turned out to be."

Just as the tears threatened to pour, she heard her sister's voice.

"Ally!" Her sister ran to her bedside and hugged her.

"I'm fine. Really. It's just a bump on the head and a cut on my knee. I'm all patched up now."

Maddie turned to the officer. "Thank you for calling me, Mr. Archer."

"No problem at all. I'll leave you two alone now." He turned and smiled. "I'll be back to see you first thing in the morning. Hope you like doughnuts."

Allison smiled back. "I do." She watched as he walked from the emergency room.

Maddie looked at her with a smirk on her lips. "What was that all about? Do you two already know each other?"

"Not before tonight. But I have a feeling I'm going to be seeing a lot more of him. It's like he doesn't believe me or something."

"Really? Well, he's probably just doing his job. He's a good guy. Lots of baggage, though. He's been through a lot, but a great man for the right woman."

"Well, I'm not her. He was only here on business. Besides, I want to put this horrible night behind me and hold my new niece."

Her words sounded nonchalant in her ears, but her body was anything but calm. It wasn't just the questions he was asking but the way he'd smiled at her and held her hand. All of it was setting off alarms. She could blame it on the concussion, but she knew better.

"Ms. Moore, we're ready to take you up to your room now. We're going to move you onto this other bed on the count of three."

Allison let the nurses help her and welcomed the soft pillow to ease the pounding in her head. As they moved her bed through the ER toward the elevators, she studied the faces of the people. Patients full of fear and family members full of worry. Most looked away as she passed by. Except for one.

A man with a long beard sitting alone in the waiting room turned to watch her as she rolled past. His dark eyes bore into hers as if he wanted to see into her soul. His large frame rose from the chair.

Was he heading straight for her?

THREE

"That's him!"

She grabbed Maddie's arm and squeezed it tight. All eyes in the emergency room were on her now.

"Allison, what is the matter with you?" Maddie whispered between clenched teeth.

The nursed pushed her bed past the waiting area and eyed her with concern. The man walked to the receptionist's desk, stopped to ask a question, then headed back to his seat. Allison felt like an idiot. Considering what she'd been through tonight, she didn't care. "That man back there," she whispered.

"Mr. Morales?"

She didn't know who Mr. Morales was, but the man in the ER looked similar to the man in the truck. Only without blood on his forehead and stains in his beard. And the tattoos on his neck. Her cheeks grew warm.

"You know him?"

Maddie nodded and shot her the same look she'd seen a million times when they were kids. A look that meant for her to stop being dramatic.

"I'm not overreacting, Maddie," she hissed.

"Allison, stop it. Mr. Morales is a sweet man. He

looks a bit rough, but he's nice. He owns the hardware store in town, and his wife owns the bakery on the highway."

"Do you know him personally?"

"Well, no, he's only an acquaintance, but I've met him through his business."

"Everything all right?"

A deep voice sounded from behind her. The slight hint of his Texas drawl was starting to sound familiar to her.

"Where did you come from? I thought you were leaving?"

He nodded in agreement. "I was. Until I heard you yelling. I was over there talking to the ER staff and asking a few more questions. I wanted to make sure no one came here injured and matching the description you gave us."

She felt ridiculous. She'd always been a little dramatic and skittish, so maybe Maddie was right. Maybe she was overreacting. She noticed how the nurse smiled at the officer as she pushed her bed into the elevator. For some odd reason, she felt irritated at the subtle, but too friendly, gesture.

"That man over there looks a lot like the man on the highway."

She watched him scan the ER waiting room. "Where?"

"I don't want to point him out, but he's standing up."

Maddie laughed. "Mr. Morales. She thinks he tried to kill her."

Embarrassment shot through her as her cheeks warmed with humiliation. "I didn't say that."

"I see." He turned to look down at her. "He does look

like a suspicious character, but so far, we've never had a complaint about him."

Allison watched as Sergeant Archer turned away and walked toward the man. Her stomach knotted. The two men talked for a minute. She watched them shake hands before the officer headed back over to her.

Maddie spoke up first. "What did he say?"

"His wife has been admitted to the ER. She thought she was having a heart attack. Being in hospitals upset him so he's waiting out here while they get her IV inserted. He also doesn't have any signs of injuries on him."

Allison glanced back at the bearded man. Her heart sank, and she mentally said a prayer for his wife.

"Going with us?" the nurse asked, her gaze fixed on the police officer.

He smiled at Allison. "No, but I'll be back tomorrow to check on you. You're safe here. Get some rest." The lighting of the hospital illuminated the green in his eyes.

Allison watched as he walked away. Maybe her sister was right. She was a mess. She closed her eyes and thought about the officer's questions. As professional as he was, she could tell he thought she was acting like a flake. Thankfully, he didn't go out of his way to make her feel like one.

Pain jarred her back to reality. Her head was killing her. All she wanted was a dark room to ease her agony and to get a good night's sleep. Maybe in the morning, this would all be a bad dream. She could only hope.

They exited the elevator, and the nurse wheeled her into a room where she'd be spending the rest of her night. Not in front of a warm fire, sipping a hot cup of coffee while getting sweet baby snuggles.

Allison pretended to listen as the nurse made her comfortable. "Try to get some sleep, Miss Moore. We'll be back to get you when radiology is ready for your MRI."

"Come on, Allison. Don't do that." Maddie frowned at her from across the room as soon as the nurse was out of sight.

"Do what?"

"You're sitting there with your arms folded, biting your lip. You're pouting."

Maddie was right. She was downright upset that her plans had gone so terribly wrong. Not to mention the fact that there was someone out there who'd tried to kill her a few hours ago.

Allison unfolded her arms. "Oh, I'm sorry. How could I be so selfish as to pout when someone has just tried to *shoot* me?"

"I'm sure they'll catch whoever did it. People can be irrational, you know that. Probably a case of road rage or maybe you startled the man. Look, I don't blame you for being scared. I'm scared, too. And disappointed. I didn't want anything to ruin our visit. I've missed you, Ally."

"This is not a random case of road rage, so stop making up stuff to try to make me feel better. It isn't working. I still think there was a dead body in that tarp."

"Come on, Allison. You're scaring yourself. What are the chances of something like that happening? Maybe you were shot at, but do you really think people carry around dead bodies in the back of their truck?"

Maddie sat on the edge of the bed eyeing her with

motherly concern. "Are you going to be okay for the night?"

Allison nodded but couldn't answer. A lump gripped her throat and choked off her words.

"Oh, Ally." Maddie moved down the side of the bed and enveloped her in a hug. "Just be thankful it all turned out the way it did. Don't think about what could've happened. God was watching over you tonight. You're safe and sound now."

"I know you're right, but it's hard to process it all. I've never been more afraid in my life."

Maddie leaned back and raised an eyebrow. "Never?"

She shrugged. "Besides that clown at my ninth birthday. You knew what I meant."

"Get some sleep. I need to get back. It's almost time for me to feed the baby. Scott can do it, but he gets so nervous. He's probably pacing the floor with her right now."

"I can't wait to meet her, Maddie."

"I know, sister. Just rest tonight. I'll be back in the morning."

She nodded her head in agreement, then leaned back in the bed and tried to pull the covers up to her neck. She gave them a firm yank. "You're on my blanket."

Maddie laughed. "How did we ever survive sharing a bed when we were kids?" She stood up and tucked the corners of the blankets back under the mattress.

"Maddie."

"Yeah?"

"Do you really think I'm overreacting? That this was just a fluke case of road rage?"

Maddie kissed her forehead. "Absolutely. Get some sleep. I'll be back to get you in the morning."

Allison watched her sister leave. Her head hurt, her stomach was in knots and she wanted to cry to purge it all from her system. She fluffed her pillow and leaned back. She closed her eyes and thanked God for keeping her safe.

The subtle whisper of breath tickled her face. She didn't know when she'd drifted off, but she was awake now, and she knew someone was watching her sleep. Her own breathing stilled. She was afraid to look. Her mouth opened to let out a scream, but fear stole her cries for help. Nothing but silence filled the room, making the soft whispering breaths tickling across her face seem like the wind of a hurricane.

He was back. And this time he was going to kill her.

"Miss Moore." A male voice cut through the silence.

Her hand flew from under the blanket and she swung wildly, hitting him in the face. "Leave me alone!" Her scream echoed through the small room.

A strong arm caught her wrist and squeezed.

"Miss Moore," he repeated with more authority.

She pulled her other arm free and hit him again in the head.

"Miss Moore!" A woman's voice called to her this time. Her eyes flew open, and she realized it was her nurse and the orderly coming to get her for the MRI.

She covered her face with her hands. "I thought you were... Never mind. I apologize. I can't believe I hit you."

"It's fine." The orderly rubbed his face with a large hand. "It's not the first time it's happened to me."

"I've told you about waking patients up like that," the nurse scolded him.

The orderly stood rubbing his face and nodding.

"Aren't you supposed to announce you're coming into the room? Or turn on a light? Something?"

The orderly laughed. "Next time I will. Lesson learned."

"I'm sorry I hit you."

"Don't worry about it. You do have a mean right hook." He took a defensive stance with his fists in the air.

She laughed and lay back down as they wheeled her out of the room. Her sister was right, as usual. She was a mess.

He stood in the doorway of her room, holding a box of doughnuts as he watched her sleep. She was a beautiful woman. The fact that he thought so made him uneasy. The quicker he got the answers he came for, the better off he'd be.

Jackson entered the room and walked to her bed. He reached out to set the doughnuts on the tray next to her. He stumbled backward when her eyes flew open. A fist flew from under the blanket.

"Whoa, there."

Her eyes were big and full of fear. She looked at him for a few seconds, then let out a sigh. He felt awful for startling her while she slept.

"What are you doing back here so soon?"

He set the box of doughnuts on her tray. He had a lot of reasons for coming back to talk to her, but he needed to start slowly. "It's already morning."

It was unclear how bad her concussion was. She'd been unconscious for a few minutes, and he couldn't risk waiting to see if amnesia would set in or not. He needed answers before the memories became lost in her mind forever. Head injuries had a weird way of affecting people.

"Is there anything new you may have remembered about last night?"

She bit her lip. "I think I've told you everything. I don't see what more I could tell you. Have you found the man who shot at me?"

"No." It was a relief that she wasn't showing any signs of memory loss. "I'm sorry, but I have a few more questions."

"You need to ask them this morning?"

"Unfortunately, yes."

"Like I told you, I was shot at. I ran off the road, hit my head, I'm here, blah, blah."

He wanted to laugh at her sarcasm because it reminded him so much of himself.

"Yes, ma'am, I know that part. I need to know if there's anyone who can validate the time you left your house to drive here. Did you make any stops along the way?"

Her eyes widened. "What are you asking me this for?"

"It's my job to ask questions, Miss Moore. Don't take any offense to it. Where do you work?"

He studied her reactions carefully. He really wanted to believe her story. He wanted to believe she had nothing to hide.

"I work at Paradigm Enterprises as Avery Guerrero's personal assistant."

"And just what is it you do?"

"Everything. I probably know more about his company than he does."

"What exactly is Paradigm Enterprises?"

"That's the corporate name. He owns several restaurants and a couple of luxury hotels in Texas and Louisiana. He got his start in the restaurant business. Have you heard of Bordelon's?"

He'd more than heard of it. It was a fancy place to eat that carried an expensive tab. He'd taken Natalie there on their third anniversary. "Of course. So, what do you really do?"

"I told you, everything."

"Can you be more specific?"

She let out a long sigh. "Well, I set up his appointments and send out his emails. I also answer his phone and keep up with the day-to-day correspondence. He doesn't like to shop, so I schedule his meals and do his shopping. When he asks, I schedule his haircut appointments and whatever else he needs me to do."

He held up a hand. "Sorry. I get it. Does his wife do anything for him?"

"I don't know anything about his wife. She doesn't come to the office. He keeps her out of his business. He said something once about not mixing personal affairs with business. It made me think that he doesn't care to have her in that part of his life."

"Do they know what time you left work yesterday?"

"No, the office was closed yesterday."

"Why was that?"

Allison shrugged. "It was odd, but not uncommon for Avery. He said he wasn't feeling well and told me to take the day off, too."

"Where do you live?"

"Houston. I rent an apartment in the Heights. I've been there for about five years."

He wrote down what she was telling him. He was

eager to ask his next question. "Any boyfriend or significant other who knows when you left?"

"No, no one. I live alone. I called Maddie after I got on the highway. She's the only person I talked to yesterday." She shifted in her bed and stared at him with narrowed eyes. "I know there's something you're not telling me."

He continued to scribble in his notebook. She was right. There was a lot he wasn't telling her. Couldn't tell her. He watched as she pulled her long hair back from her face, twisted it in a knot on top of her head, then let it fall. It cascaded over her shoulders like satin.

"Hey, are you ready to get out of here?" Her sister popped her head into the room and waited a second before stepping inside.

"Are you kidding? I've been ready. The doctor said the MRI was clear. I'm good to go. They're bringing my discharge papers within the hour."

The door opened again. A male nurse started to walk into the room but looked at the three of them and stopped.

"I didn't know you had visitors. I'll come back. The doctor wanted me to give you some pain medicine this morning."

"I thought I was going home."

"I'm sure you are." He was already backing out of the room. "I'll be back in a little while."

Jackson thought he was acting weird, but sometimes people did that around cops.

"I'm heading to the station. I'll be in touch if the detectives need more information from you. Glad to see you're not dealing with any lasting effects from the concussion."

He turned to her sister. "Maddie, my nephew sure will be glad when you come back to school."

"Thank you. Tell him I'll be back soon. My maternity leave will end in three weeks."

He smiled at them both and turned to leave. Something made him glance back. The second he did, their eyes locked. Before Allison could notice the heat creeping into his cheeks, he turned and shut the door.

Her sister was the one person in this world she could count on. It was a comfort to have family around her, especially after the past few months. Having a fiancé cheat on you with your best friend was a blow most women didn't get over quickly. In her twenty-six years, she hadn't found a man she could totally trust. Maddie was blessed to find Scott. Her brother-in-law was one of a kind. He cooked, cleaned, took his family to church and was ruggedly handsome. Scott also owned a successful construction company and provided well for her sister and nieces. Allison was glad at least one of them had found true love.

"I really wish they would hurry up and let me leave. I'm dying to see my niece. How is Charlotte doing?"

"She's the best baby. She hardly ever cries. Which is a good thing, because Phoebe cried constantly. She didn't sleep through the night until she was three years old. Hopefully, Charlotte will stay as sweet as she is right now."

Listening to her sister talk about the girls made her heart ache. The long-awaited weekend was turning into a pure nightmare. "It feels so unfair that I'm having to deal with this."

"It's life, Ally. Things happen." She glanced at her

watch. "I need to get back to feed Charlotte. My friend is watching the girls because Scott had to go back to work today. I'm going to go see if I can find out how much longer we'll be here."

"Thank you. You're the best."

Allison laid her head back on the pillow and watched a rerun of one of her favorite childhood shows. The television was muted, but she'd seen the episode so many times she knew all the words. She yawned and fought to keep her eyes open. She was still a little drowsy from all the pain medicine and stress. Her eyes closed and her body began to relax.

A sound jarred her awake. She noticed the door to her room moving. A different male nurse than the one who'd walked in her room earlier stood at the side of her bed. "Here's your pain medicine. Maybe now you can take it."

She sat up and took the pill from his hand. She noticed he didn't put it in a paper cup like the other nurse had done, and he didn't go to the computer to log it in. He didn't check her bracelet this time, either. But what did she know? She wasn't a nurse and hated hospitals. She hadn't been in one since she was a kid, and she'd prayed to never go back. Still, she had to ask why he'd overlooked what seemed to be an important detail.

"Why didn't you check my bracket and enter the drugs on the computer the way the other nurse did?"

His brow creased as he shoved the pill at her. She'd insulted him.

"I took care of everything while I was waiting on your visitors to leave. I do have other patients besides you." His tone sounded irritated.

"Oh." She looked at the medicine in her hand. It

looked exactly like the other ones she'd been given, but after all she'd been through, she wasn't about to trust him. She took the cup of water he offered and smiled. She pretended to put it into her mouth, then drank the water.

He watched her for a second and then stepped toward the bed. "Are you sure you swallowed it?"

Her nerves were on edge now. What kind of question was that? She wasn't a child. She opened her mouth so he could see.

He laughed under his breath and glanced back toward the door. He pulled a syringe from his pocket and grabbed her wrist. The pill fell to the floor. Before she could scream, he plunged the needle deep into her arm. "You'll be leaving here before you know it. But you'll be in a body bag."

What had he given her? Her eyes began to blur. She saw a shadowy figure leave the room. Her body felt weak, then numb, almost as if she were floating above herself. Something was happening to her. Something awful.

She tried to push the call button on the bed, but her fingers kept missing it. After several tries, her index finger found the button. She couldn't tell if she'd pushed it hard enough to make the call. What was happening to her? *Dear Lord, please don't let me die.*

She could hardly make out Maddie running into her room with a nurse. She was in a dark tunnel and she couldn't hear anything. Was Maddie screaming at her?

"Shh…" She fought to say the word again. "Shh…"

"Allison, I can't understand you!" Maddie yelled.

"Shot," she whispered, then the lights went out.

FOUR

Jackson headed to his desk with his third cup of coffee. He hoped he'd have time to enter a few reports on the computer before going home. Leaning back in his chair, he rubbed his temples. His head ached and his vision blurred. The last meal he'd eaten was at lunch the day before. He knew he needed to take better care of himself. Over the past five years, he'd learned he could get by without a lot of things. Sleep and food being a couple of them. His stomach rumbled from all the caffeine he'd already had.

"Hey, Jackson. Got a minute?"

The look on Devon's face said it all. "Sure. What you got?"

"You're not going to believe me when I tell you. Hey, I need one of those."

Jackson handed him the half-full foam cup he'd just poured for himself.

Devon frowned and set it down. "Can't you get a rookie to make us a decent pot of coffee?"

Jackson glanced at O'Neil, who was already making his way to the break room. The young cop grabbed the coffee cup from the desk without saying a word, then walked away.

"What'd you find?"

Devon waited until he was sure O'Neil was out of hearing distance. "We got an ID back on the dead body. Sierra Wolfe. She's a fed."

"Oh, man."

"DEA to be exact. No one had heard from her in a couple of days. The DEA got worried and put out a BOLO on her undercover vehicle. That earring you found was hers. What that guy did her…it was horrible."

"I know what they did. I saw her. Who do they think could have done it?"

"Don't know. She was married, but no kids. The license plate on the truck was stolen off a car in Austin, so we can at least pinpoint the truck to that area. We've got more questions than answers right now. What information do you have on the woman who called it in?"

"Allison Moore. Works for Avery Guerrero at Paradigm Enterprises. No husband, no kids. She was headed to her sister's house for the weekend. She's in the hospital waiting to be discharged today."

"Don't let her get too far away. Depending on what the lab sends us back, we might be bringing her in."

"I can tell by the way she's acting that she's not guilty of anything. She's scared out of her mind right now."

"Maybe."

"What's that supposed to mean?" His irritation was thick, and it shocked him that he felt it. He didn't know why he needed to protect a perfect stranger.

Devon fired back. "Do you know this woman or something?"

"No. Never met her before in my life."

"Maybe she's an accomplice. Look, until I get that DNA test back, she's not innocent. Or guilty. So far, she's the only person we have who was in the same place as the body. Come on, Jackson. You know how this works."

He did. He'd been in law enforcement a long time. Before Hope died, he'd wanted to be a detective. Now he didn't know what he wanted.

Jackson felt a firm hand land on his shoulder. He turned to see Captain Rusty Schmille standing over him.

"Hey, Cap."

Jackson did his best to fake some enthusiasm. Something about Rusty had always irritated him. He despised all the dumb jokes and he thought he was the worst captain he'd ever worked under, but that was only a matter of opinion.

"What are you guys following up on?"

Jackson explained the gist of his night on duty and waited for Rusty's reaction.

"Sierra Wolfe, huh? Never heard of her. How'd they know it was her so quickly?"

Devon shrugged. "DEA had already sent us a BOLO on her car with a photo of her. We were able to get some prints from the body and matched them with her profile in the DEA's database. It's not rocket science, Cap."

Jackson fought back a grin as Schmille's ears ignited a shade of scarlet. This guy could dish it out but he sure couldn't take it.

"All right, you goons. If you're done making a clown out of me, go find out who did this and see if that woman in the hospital can ID this man. If she can't, let her go. You don't need her to work this case. If we have any suspects, we'll call her."

"No can do," Devon said.

"Why not?"

"Her DNA could be on the truck, and we don't have that test back yet."

As Rusty opened his mouth to refute his friend, O'Neil shouted from across the room. "Jackson, you've got a call. She said her name is Maddie Porter."

Devon raised an eyebrow. "Girlfriend?"

"'Bout time, Jackson. I was beginning to take you for a recluse." Rusty laughed as he walked away.

"Grow up. Both of you. She's the sister of the woman in the hospital."

Jackson reached for the phone on the corner of his desk. "This is Jackson Archer."

"Jackson, someone tried to kill Allison. She's in ICU."

Jackson's heart slammed his chest. "On my way!" He stood up, and Devon stood with him.

"I'm going with you. You can tell me what happened on the way." Devon was right on his heels.

"Someone tried to kill her."

"Great. Our only witness and she might be dead, too."

Jackson glared at Devon. Cops had a way of becoming calloused, and he knew it wasn't a personal statement. He didn't know this woman, but something about her had gotten to him.

They made their way to the police car. Devon buckled his seat belt and stared at the photo lying on the seat. Jackson shrugged a shoulder.

"It's been a long time since I've seen a picture of

her," Devon said. He picked it up and studied it. "This case has haunted me every single day. I'd give anything to find who did it."

Jackson's temper reached a tipping point, and he snatched the picture from Devon's hand. He shoved it back into its spot under the sun visor.

"Sorry. Don't take it personally."

"I never do." Devon stared out the window.

They drove on for a few minutes in silence. Devon spoke up first.

"I hope this woman is able to talk when we get there. Did her sister say anything else? I can't believe someone tried to kill her in the hospital."

"You know as much as I do. Things are escalating quickly, and I'm getting little worried for this woman's safety."

"I get that, but I'm kind of starting to worry about you lately."

"I'm fine."

Devon put up a hand. "I'm just asking."

"Well, don't."

"Come on, Jackson. We've been good friends for a long time. I promised Hope I'd always look after you."

"You don't have to babysit me, Devon. I'm doing okay."

"I know. I just miss hanging out with you. When is the last time you met us for bowling on Thursday? And you turned me down the last time I invited you hunting. It's like…you quit on life, Jackson. I worry about you sometimes."

The honesty of his words cut deep, but he'd learned how to ignore the pain.

"I appreciate you worrying about me, but you don't have to. I'm doing great."

Devon nodded and stared out the side window. "Yeah, okay. Just know the invitation still stands whenever you're ready."

He knew Devon was right, but he wasn't going to talk about it. It was true that he didn't know how to live anymore. He'd accepted the fact that Hope and his baby girl were gone. He knew nothing would bring them back. But going to church? Being happy? He still couldn't quit blaming God for taking the two best things that had ever happened to him. What on earth did he have to be happy about?

Jackson pulled into the ER entrance. As they raced toward the sliding glass doors, he braced himself for what was about to happen. A strong urge to pray for her nagged at him, but he ignored it. She would either live or die. Praying wasn't going to make a difference at this point, anyway. It hadn't helped his wife and child. It wouldn't help Allison, either.

Jackson asked the ER receptionist where to find Allison, then they headed upstairs to the trauma floor. He wasn't prepared for what he saw when he approached the ICU cubicle.

Allison lay motionless while a doctor monitored her breathing and heartbeat with a stethoscope. He finished and walked toward them. "Can I help you?"

Jackson extended his hand. "I'm Sergeant Jackson Archer and this is Detective Devon Sparks."

"Dr. Larry Winston."

"Do you mind if we ask you some questions, Dr. Winston?" Jackson half expected him to say no.

"Sure, go ahead. But I've only got a few minutes."

"Thank you. Can you tell us what happened?"

"All I can tell you is that when her sister found her, she was pretty close to dead. Her breathing was labored, heart rate had dropped, blood pressure was low. Her pupils were pinpoints. She was able to tell her sister a few words before she lost consciousness. She mentioned a shot. Based on the symptoms she was presenting, we gave her Naloxone to reverse the drug. The lab is running tests right now, but I'm pretty sure she was given a large dose of morphine. She responded almost immediately to the antidote, but she's very fortunate to be alive. She's sleeping now, and her vitals are doing remarkably well considering what she's been through."

Jackson let Devon take the lead with the questioning.

"Who was the nurse on duty? I'm going to need the names of everyone who went into that room."

"Unfortunately, accidents do happen, gentlemen. Hospital administrators are on their way down to talk to you. But like I said, I only have a few minutes and they're up right about now."

Jackson didn't like the doctor's tone or attitude. "That's unfortunate, Doc. Look, we get that this is throwing your day off. A woman was almost murdered in this hospital, and it's our job to find out what happened. I think whatever you have in your schedule can hold for a few more minutes. Don't you?"

His demeanor quickly changed. "I apologize. I haven't slept or had anything to eat, so I'm feeling some burnout right now."

Jackson brought his own tone down a few notches. The doctor was talking about something they could relate to. "We totally understand that feeling. Why don't you let Detective Sparks take you to get a cup of coffee and a bite to eat and you can answer his questions?"

The doctor nodded. "Sure, I guess I can do that. But only for a few minutes. I have to finish my rounds and get some sleep."

Jackson heard Allison's voice from behind him. They all turned around to see Maddie standing over her bed. A flutter went through his stomach.

"What's going on?" Her head turned in their direction.

Jackson ignored the fact that his heartbeat sped up when she looked at him. This time, he didn't try to hide what he was feeling. His mind whispered a thankful prayer that she was alive.

Allison fought to open her eyes. Her mouth was dry and her body felt weak. "What happened?"

"Allison! Oh, thank God." Maddie leaned down and hugged her shoulders. She pulled back and kissed her forehead.

"Someone tell me what happened." She wondered if she was awake or if this was a dream. Her brain was still foggy.

"Allison, I'm Dr. Winston. It seems someone gave you the wrong medication. You're going to be fine now. Just relax and rest. You'll need to stay in the hospital a little longer, but you're doing great."

"What? No!" This couldn't be happening. She was leaving. She didn't care what they were talking about. They'd promised to let her go today and she was going.

She fought to sit up in the bed. "There's been a mistake. I was about to be discharged."

She noticed Jackson and another officer. "Why are you here?"

After a few seconds, Allison processed what the doctor had told her. Had someone given her the wrong medication on purpose?

The nurse! He came into her room without checking the medicine into the computer. How could she have been so stupid to trust him? He had given her a shot of something.

"Someone tried to kill me again. Maddie, I'm getting out of here." She threw the blankets back and tried to swing a leg over the edge of the bed. Her body betrayed her. She held the bedrail when the room began to spin.

"Ally, calm down. We don't know that for sure. Just rest and get better so you can come home with me and see the kids." Maddie smoothed the hair out of her eyes with her fingers. Allison grabbed her wrist.

"Listen to me. Someone came into my room and gave me a pill. He didn't log it in. He told me he did, but he didn't. When I questioned him, he said the pill was for pain. I realized he didn't log it into the computer, so I asked about that, too. That's when he got irritated. He asked me to show him that I swallowed it."

She felt around in the bed. Her hand brushed over the pill she'd pretended to take. "Here it is!"

"Let me see it. We'll be needing that for evidence." Jackson stuck out his hand.

She gave him the pill and continued with her story. "As soon as I opened my mouth, he grabbed my arm and gave me a shot. I started to feel weird and then I passed out."

"Can you remember what he looked like?" Jackson asked.

Maddie spoke up first. "I saw him. He came in while I was still here. He was tall, heavyset, broad shoulders. His hair and eyes were dark."

Allison nodded in agreement. "Exactly like that."

"Maddie, stay with her. I'm going to go talk to administrators and pull some surveillance video. Don't let her out of your sight." Devon walked toward the door.

Maddie cleared her throat, then said, "Of course. I need to make a quick call. I keep getting texts from my mother-in-law asking me where the extra milk is. She's wants to know how much longer until I get there. I'm not sure if she's got everything under control or not. It's starting to worry me."

Her sister was babbling. Maddie always did that when she was nervous. Allison sighed and fought back the tears threatening to spill down her cheeks. This was all getting worse instead of better.

"What's wrong?" Maddie asked.

"Nothing. I came here to see my nieces, and look at the mess that's happened to me. I'm sick of it. For once in my life I wish something would go right."

"Shh. You're starting to yell, Allison." Maddie patted her hand.

She didn't mean to raise her voice, but her emotions were raging.

"You'll be out of here soon. Just be patient." Maddie kissed her forehead and shot Jackson a look.

"I'm going to step out for a second. Scott's mom is a worrier, so I really need to call her."

She was alone with Jackson in the ICU. He paced the floor at the foot of her bed. It was an irritating gesture that made her both nervous and angry. "Please, sit down."

Jackson shot her an incredulous glare. The firm set in his jaw and creased eyebrow left no doubt what he was thinking. She was grateful when he walked over to a chair in the corner and sat. Fatigue showed on his face, but it didn't distract from his handsome looks.

Allison picked up a clear cup of water from her bed-side tray and caught a glimpse of her reflection. There was no telling what he must think of her appearance.

"I'm sorry. My nerves are on edge." Allison tried to ease the tension between them.

"No, it's fine. It's a bad habit."

"My attitude?"

He laughed. "No, the pacing. I do it when I'm ner-vous, angry, bored. Or whenever I'm cooped up in a tiny space like this."

"I feel the same way right now. Only I'm not allowed out of this bed."

Devon walked in without saying a word. His eyes met Jackson's, and they looked at each other as if they knew some deep, dark secret that she didn't.

Devon turned to her. "Are you ready to go?"

Finally, someone was making sense. "Now that is a man with a plan. I'm ready when you are."

"Did the doctor clear her?" Jackson stood up.

"Doesn't matter. We need to get her out of here ASAP." He winked at her. "She's been here long enough."

Something in Devon's tone told her he wasn't really joking around. This was serious.

"What is it? What's going on?"

"Nothing. We're just getting you out of here."

She wasn't buying it. "My sister is here. Why can't I go home with her?"

Devon shook his head. "No. I know this isn't making sense to you, but we'll tell you everything when the time is right. We're going to get you to a safe house until this mess is resolved."

A safe house? Her stomach felt like it was sliding out of her body.

Jackson turned to her. "Allison, you're going to have to trust us."

She didn't miss the look the two men gave each other. Trust was something she wasn't good at. As much as she wanted to, she couldn't. Not yet. The room felt uneven and heat warmed her hands. The beating of her heart slammed the inside of her chest like a sledgehammer.

Her life was really in danger.

And they knew it.

FIVE

Jackson helped Allison sit up on the edge of the bed. He didn't know much about being a doctor, but she didn't appear to be ready to leave the hospital yet. A morphine overdose had to be a hard thing to bounce back from, but somehow, she made it seem like a cakewalk. Allison was a tough woman. She reminded him so much of Hope. Not one thing about their physical appearance was the same, but something about her brave determination made them a lot alike. Hope would've liked her.

Devon narrowed his eyes in Jackson's direction, then took control of the conversation. "Jackson will take you to a safe place. You'll need to hurry. After we get you secured, we'll explain to you what's going on. For now, let's take care of one thing at a time."

He watched her face while Devon told her the plan. She didn't flinch. She sat on the edge of the bed listening and nodding. He wasn't sure if she understood that her life was in real danger, but she was handling it well.

"What about my nieces? I haven't seen them yet."

"All right, then. We're ready. You'll need to get dressed now," Devon said. He ignored her question.

She looked around the small space and smiled. "You need to give me some privacy, boys."

An unexpected heat warmed Jackson's cheeks. He pulled the curtain around her bed, and he and Devon stepped to the other side. A few minutes later, Allison pulled the curtain back and stood before them wearing a pair of jeans and a T-shirt. Even in those casual clothes she looked gorgeous.

"I'm ready." She grabbed the side of the bed to steady herself.

Jackson looked around the ICU for a wheelchair. He motioned toward the nurses' station. "Can we get a wheelchair?"

Within seconds, a nurse found them one. They pushed Allison down the hallway toward the exit.

Devon pulled his phone from his pocket. "Jackson, I'll meet up with you in a little while. I'll call O'Neil to come pick me up and take me back to the station. I've got some business to take care of. Stick to the plan and I'll see you both in a few hours." He smiled at Allison. "Make sure you get some rest. We promised the doctors we'd take good care of you."

She smiled back and Jackson's stomach tightened.

"Thank you," she said.

Jackson pushed her into the elevator and leaned against the wall when the doors shut.

She covered her face with her hands.

"Are you all right?" His heart shattered. This poor woman had been through a lot since he'd first met her last night.

She shook her head in denial. He put a hand on her shoulder. "I won't let anything happen to you."

She didn't answer. The doors opened and he pushed

her out of the elevator. She sat with her hands still covering her face. They exited the emergency room doors and headed to his cruiser parked out front. He helped her get in and waved down a nurse who was leaving the hospital.

"Would you mind returning this for me?" He rolled the wheelchair to the sidewalk, not waiting for an answer. He climbed into the car and pulled away. The air inside the car was freezing. As refreshing as it was for him, he was sure it was too cold for her. He cranked up the heater and reached into the back seat. He handed her his heavy coat. She smiled and covered up with it. An awkward silence hung between them. No matter how hard he wracked his brain, he didn't know what to say to her. What do you say to a woman whose life had been turned upside down in the blink of an eye?

Nothing. That's what. Just like no one could change the fate of his life that horrible night years ago. No words could make it better.

"I'm sorry, I'm still shaken up," she finally said. "I don't know what to say about all of this."

At least she was as uncomfortable as he was. "You have every right to be upset. You've been through a lot the past couple of days."

She nodded. "It's not just that. It's everything. My life is a total mess. And I was so excited about this trip. I still haven't seen my nieces yet."

"I'm sorry about that. I'm not good at talking, but I'm pretty good at listening. I mean, if you need to talk or anything."

She glanced up at the picture of his family on the visor and smiled. "They're so beautiful."

His throat tightened. He looked in the rearview mirror and forced himself to ignore her comment. That wasn't a topic he wanted to discuss.

"How old is she?"

There were a lot of things he hated to talk about, but there was nothing he detested more than having to talk about his daughter. Hope had lived a great life. She'd had experiences. She was a wife and a mother. But Natalie hadn't had a chance to live at all. In her short life she'd been a pure joy. The pain of losing her and the child Hope was carrying never left him.

He swallowed. "Three."

"She's precious. I love kids."

"She's dead."

He heard the gasp when his brutal words hit her. His stomach knotted at what he'd done. What kind of jerk was he? Who in their right mind said things like that? Maybe Devon was right about him. Somewhere along the way he'd forgotten how to be empathetic to people. He watched her turn and stare out the window. She wrapped her arms around her waist as they rode on in silence. He'd said enough. Fearful of hurting her more, he left her alone to assume the worst of him. Nothing he could say would fix what he'd done. The least he could do was apologize.

"I'm sorry. I shouldn't have been so rude."

She didn't look at him, and he didn't blame her. She stared out the window, helplessly trapped in a car with an ogre. The urge to grab her and pull her to him shocked him. He didn't know where the feelings were coming from, but they were there. Raw and unpredictable. And real. Instead, he said the only thing he could to make it right.

"Her name was Natalie. My wife's name was Hope."

She turned to look at the picture again. He could see it in her eyes. Pity that he'd gone through so much pain. He hated that look, but he'd come to realize it was all anyone could give him. And they always felt like they had to give him something to make up for his loss.

"Your wife was beautiful."

A lump lodged in his throat. In that moment, he felt compassion for her. Tact wasn't his forte, so he culled his words carefully. He didn't want to be as cruel as he'd been minutes earlier, so he spared her the truth.

"Thank you," he whispered.

"I was engaged once. It didn't quite work out."

"I'm sorry to hear that." He glanced over at her. It didn't make sense to him how anyone would let a woman like her get away.

She shook her head. "He wasn't good for me. It was a bad situation."

He knew better than ask, but as much as he tried to stop himself, he wanted to know more about her. "What happened?"

"I guess I refused to see who he really was until it was too late. I've learned to move on and get past it. I have faith that God will send me the right man when it's time. But I do have scars from it."

He stopped at a red light and turned to face her. Regret flowed over him for asking her to talk about it. Unlike him, she was being kind about it.

She pointed ahead. "The light is green."

After all she'd been through, her faith still seemed strong. Maybe Devon was right. He had been wallowing in self-pity for far too long. Then again, Devon had his wife and kids waiting for him at home. Devon didn't know the first thing about moving on.

He drove through the light wondering how long they would have to keep her in a safe house. As soon as this ordeal was over, he would take her to see her nieces.

"Where does your sister live?

"Sheldon Lane."

"Sheldon Lane, huh? That's a pretty nice neighborhood."

"Yeah, Scott has a really good job. Maddie doesn't have to work, but she loves teaching. She says she'll keep doing it as long as she enjoys it."

"She's a good teacher. My nephew loves her."

"She's amazing with kids. Actually, she is amazing all around. I don't know what I would've done without her. Do you have brothers and sisters around here?"

He smiled. He didn't mind talking about his brothers and the rest of his family. "Yes, I have four brothers, no sisters. My mom was a tough lady when we were growing up. She was hard as nails on us. My dad was in the army, which meant he was hard on us, too. We moved around a lot when we were kids, and my mom raised us alone during his deployments. Now we all live within fifty miles of each other. When you move around like we did, you realize that family is all you've got. We learned how to stick together."

"That's amazing. Wow, five boys. Did you fight a lot?"

He laughed. "We did. About everything."

"I like your laugh."

He could feel the heat rising from his neck. They both rode in silence for the next few minutes. Not a single woman since Hope had made his cheeks flush. Irritated with his own thoughts, he broke the awkward silence.

"Is it just you and your sister?"

"We had a brother, too."

"What do you mean?"

"He was older than us." She turned and looked out the window. "He died when he was thirteen. It was an ATV accident. He was at a friend's house when it happened. My parents never got over it, but they forgave the other kid's parents for not supervising them. I'm sure you know..." She let her words linger.

He knew what she was going to say. He knew exactly how her parents felt. "I don't know what to say. I'm sorry." As much as he hated those words when spoken to him, it was all he had to offer her. "How did you and your family get through it? I'm sure it was hard on you being a kid and all."

"With God. I grew up in church. Our church family stepped in and helped us out a lot. People brought meals, mowed our lawn and helped my parents plan the funeral. I remember Maddie sitting with me at night. She used to sit on the edge of my bed and pray with me. The only answer I can give you is that God carried us through it."

Jackson frowned. That's where he would let the conversation end. He was raised in church, too, but when God allowed Hope, Natalie, and his unborn son to die, that's when he and God had parted ways. What kind of God let something like that happen? He'd arrested criminals who'd abused their wives, girlfriends and children, but they still had their families.

And he didn't.

God hadn't done him any personal favors lately, but Jackson was glad He'd helped Allison through her loss. She was a sweet girl who'd been through way too much.

"I can tell you have doubts about what I just said."
Her tone was gentle but accusatory.

He started to say something but closed his mouth.
She'd almost read his mind, but this was one conversation he wasn't going to have today. Or ever.

It wasn't as if she blamed him for doubting God's
love and mercy. The amount of pain in his life was more
than some people would ever know.

She turned back to him. "I'm not trying to tell you
how to feel. I hope that's not what it sounds like."

He nodded. "No hard feelings. Besides, I owe you
an apology. I'm not being very honest with you about
myself. I don't know why I'm even talking to you about
this, because I don't ever talk about it. My wife and my
daughter are both gone. Killed in a car accident on the
highway about five years ago."

Her heart shattered. She recalled the two beautiful
faces in the picture, and tears burned her eyes. Saying
she was sorry seemed trite and unnecessary. This man
had been through a tremendous amount of pain and still
gave his life to serving others. She watched him rake a
hand though his hair and pretend to check his rearview
mirror to avoid making eye contact with her.

"Thank you for telling me. I promise not to make
you talk about it ever again. Unless you want to, and
then I'll only listen."

"Not many people afford me that luxury. Most people try to make me talk about it."

"I know what you mean. When my fiancé and I
broke up, people thought it was their right to know
what happened. Which is why I feel bad for asking
you so many questions that are none of my business."

She reached out to touch his forearm. He flinched and turned to face her. Her hand froze in midair inches away from his arm. She pulled back.

"How about we start over?" she asked.

His body relaxed and he nodded. "I can agree to that."

Jackson's cell phone rang. Allison watched as he answered.

"Archer."

Her heart pounded as she saw his expression turn serious. He hung up after a few seconds and smiled at her.

Relief rushed through her body. "Everything okay?"

"Oh, yeah." He shrugged a shoulder. "Nothing's changed."

They rode the next few miles in silence until his phone rang again. With the phone clenched to his face, he scanned the road, turning to look in all directions.

"Got it." He threw the phone onto the seat.

Allison's heart raced. She wanted to go back home to Houston and start the whole weekend over. She wanted out of this nightmare.

Jackson glanced in the rearview mirror every few seconds.

"What's wrong? Please don't tell me it's nothing. I can see that it's serious by the way you're acting. What was that call about?"

He opened his mouth, then shut it.

"Who was that on the phone? Was it Devon?"

Jackson let out a short breath.

"Yes. Now stay down and keep your face away from the window."

SIX

Jackson winced at the crass sound of his words. He intentionally changed his tone. "Stay calm and listen." He glanced in the side mirror, then back at her. He noticed tears on her cheeks. "Hey, are you all right?"

"Yes," she whispered on a ragged breath. "Just disappointed. I came all this way to see my family and now this is happening."

He touched her arm. "I'm only trying to keep you safe." He moved his hand and fixed his attention back to the road.

"What about Maddie and her family? Are they safe?"

He nodded. "They're safe. I promise when this is all over, I'll get you to see those nieces of yours."

"There's something you and Detective Sparks aren't telling me. Don't you think I have the right to know what's going on?"

The truth was that she'd stumbled onto something dangerous. Someone was out to get her for what she'd seen. Allison was right. She deserved some answers, but he wasn't being told everything, either. It was impossible to give her the answers she needed.

"Sergeant Archer, I want to know everything. Please."

He nodded. "I'm taking you to a safe house, but I can't tell you where we're going. We're doing this because we have reason to believe you're in real danger. You understand that you saw something you shouldn't have seen, right? We're still learning about this case, so that's all I can tell you for now. They're not telling me everything, either. Don't feel like you're the only one in the dark about the details."

"I think it's time for me to get out of this town. I'm going back home to Houston, or maybe I'll visit my parents in New Mexico. If you can help me get a rental car tomorrow, I'll be out of here and this whole thing will be over."

The retort wasn't expected. His head whipped around to face her. "Absolutely not."

She shot him a look that said she wasn't backing down.

"Why not?"

"You'd be dead by sundown."

She inhaled to make up for the air that his words had knocked out of her. This wasn't making any sense.

"Why would you say that?"

"Because it's true."

"You're not telling me everything. What is so terrible that I can't know? It's my life that's in danger. Don't you think you owe it to me? I deserve the truth. I get that I witnessed something bad, but what I want to know is why someone wants me dead? I'm a nobody. I'm no threat to anyone." She crossed her arms. "I don't care what you say. I'm leaving tomorrow."

The lines of his jaw tightened. She'd hit a nerve. He opened his mouth to reply and stopped when his cell phone rang again. He glared at her as he picked it up and tapped it on. "Go ahead."

Allison stayed quiet, straining to make out the voice on the line, but she couldn't decipher the words. She laid her head back on the seat and closed her eyes. Anger and fear seethed in her chest. She needed to relax and think rationally.

Dear God, please keep me safe. Help me figure out what to do.

The clean scent of his car air freshener filled her senses as she forced herself to remain calm. She kept her eyes closed as he continued to talk. The smell of his woodsy cologne mingled with the air freshener.

Tears burned her eyes, and she dared them not to fall. She wasn't about to start crying in front of him. It wasn't like this was the first bad thing that had ever happened to her. She'd always considered herself a strong woman, but getting shot at and poisoned was putting her resilience to the test.

Jackson put his phone on the seat and let out a long sigh. His shoulders slumped, and for a minute she thought he looked defeated.

"What is it?" she asked. She dreaded his answer.

"Nothing." He straightened up in the seat and smiled.

His tone didn't convince her. "I'm sorry I'm acting so short with you. I know you're only doing your job, but I feel so helpless."

He looked at her with those intense viridescent eyes. "I know. Don't worry about it."

She turned toward the window to hide her face from him. "Why this is happening to me? It's not as if my life was in a great place or anything, but things were going well. I love my job, but how can I be sure I'll have one when I go home? Avery has always been good to me. Maybe he will understand after I explain everything." She sighed. "I want my old life back. I was finally in a good place after dealing with my ex. I was picking myself up and moving on. My life was better than I'd realized."

Allison turned to look at him. "I'll be more cooperative from now on."

"Really, it's fine. I'm used to it. I've dealt with people who are a lot meaner than you." He grinned and winked at her.

"I stopped on the road to help someone. I thought I was doing the right thing. I guess helping people is the wrong thing to do around here."

"Helping people is never the wrong thing to do."

"Did you always want to be a police officer?"

"I don't think so. I remember wanting to be a professional baseball player when I was a little kid. Then reality set in, and I figured I had to set my sights on something a little more attainable."

"Understandable. I think every little boy wants to play professional sports of some sort."

He nodded in agreement. "What about you? What did you want to be when you were a kid?"

She thought about her reply and shrugged a shoulder. It wasn't that it was embarrassing to admit, but at this point it was unattainable.

"Come on, every kid knows what they want to be when you grow up. Don't be embarrassed."

"A mom."

Silence blanketed them. Jackson drove the next ten

minutes without saying a word. She was thankful for the lack of conversation, but she knew he didn't press because he didn't want to hear what she had to say. She tried not to bring it up around people, especially her sister. Maddie always changed the subject or acted like she didn't want to hear about it. It was obvious her sister carried guilt for being able to conceive her own children. Allison didn't hold any jealousy. It was her burden to bear, not her sister's. And in the years since getting the bad news, she'd done a pretty good job of dealing with it. Now that she thought about it, she'd always been able to handle anything that happened to her. Not that life was easy, but putting her trust in God hadn't failed her yet.

"How many kids do you want?"

The question shattered the silence. She hadn't talked about it for years and wasn't sure she was ready to now, but she'd brought it up. She picked at some flaking nail polish on her index finger as she searched for the right words.

"I would feel blessed to have just one, if I could."

"I'm sorry. We don't have to talk about this." His tone was gentle and understanding.

"It's okay. I don't mind. The doctors aren't sure if I'll be able to conceive. But I know that if it's God's will, it will happen. I have to put my faith in Him."

It was the first time in years she'd been willing to talk about it with anyone other than her family. He shifted behind the steering wheel and she braced for his response.

"I'm sorry. Let's talk about something else." He raked a hand through his hair. Emotionally charged conversations were something he obviously avoided.

She shrugged, hoping to appear nonchalant. "It's okay. Bad things happen to good people. Maddie always told me that when we were young. She said, 'Allison, bad things happen to good people all the time. God is your strength, and He can get you through anything you face. You're smart, beautiful and funny, and you're going to do great things with your life.'" Allison smiled to herself. "And you know what—I actually believed her."

"She's right. You're a strong woman. Stronger than I am."

She scoffed. "No, I'm not. I'm scared to death right now. I have no idea how I got into this mess. Or how I'll get out of it."

"I don't know how you did, either. I guess it goes back to what your sister said about bad things happening to good people."

"You should take your own advice."

"Yeah, well, no one said I was good people."

She shot him a worried look and then stared back down at her phone. It bothered her that he didn't have a better opinion of himself, but she knew it was because of all he'd lost.

"Do you think my sister and her family are going to be okay?"

"I'm sure they are. Whoever is after you probably isn't concerned about your sister. You're the one they're after, not her. A patrol officer will be in their neighborhood to give you both some peace of mind."

"What about my parents? Can I call them? Or at least send them a text message?"

"No, that's not a good idea right now."

"Why not? I hope they're not in any danger." Her voice shook at the thought of not being able to talk to them. It wasn't as if she was going to defy his advice, but she needed to know what danger she was putting her parents in, if any. If something happened to her family because of her, she'd never forgive herself.

"Let's get you safe first, and then you can call your parents. It won't hurt anything to call them. Just don't tell them where you are."

"And where would that be?"

"I can't tell you that, but you'll be safe."

All she wanted was her life back. Her boring, predictable life. She picked up her phone and opened the photo app to look at the pictures Maddie had sent her of the baby. Seeing that precious face would make her feel better. Allison scrolled through her photos.

"What in the world?" She inhaled sharply. Her hand shook as she held the phone closer to her face.

"What's wrong?"

"This picture." She held the phone up so he could see it.

He glanced quickly as he drove. "Who is that?"

"It's him!"

"Him who?"

"The man in the truck," she said, shaking the phone.

"How'd you get that? Do you already know him?"

"No, I didn't realize I had taken this picture. It must've happened when I was trying to use my phone to shine light into the truck."

Without warning, Jackson pulled the cruiser over and took the phone from her. He studied it carefully. A grave expression covered his face.

"Are you sure that's when you took this? And you don't know who this is?"

"I'd never forget that tattoo on his neck. It sent chills

down my back as soon as my light hit it. Who tattoos a woman's face on their neck?"

"I've seen a few." Jackson enlarged the picture to get a better look. His stomach clenched. He recognized this man. He was a member of the cartel, and he was wanted for murder.

He picked up his cell and made a call. "Hey, Devon, I'm going to send you a picture. She found it on her phone."

He hung up and forwarded the picture from her phone to Devon's email address. He handed it back to her. "Don't erase any pictures or change anything on your phone in case we need it."

"What's going on?"

"I don't know yet. I'll tell you as soon as Devon gets back to me. I need you to try to remember anything else you can about that night."

She closed her eyes and tried to put the events in order. "I remember seeing a flash in the cab of the truck when I bent down to ask if anyone needed help. That must've been when I took the picture. After that I heard the bullets ricochet off the rocks."

Jackson pulled in a breath, then released it. "If this is what I think it is, some really bad people are looking for you. They won't stop until you're dead."

SEVEN

Jackson regretted his last statement. He'd been blunt to tell her that her death was a certainty now if these people found her. It wasn't his intention to scare her, but his rotten mood was taking over all aspects of his life. Even if he didn't like what this beautiful woman was doing to him, he didn't have the right to make her feel bad. If Hope was still alive, she wouldn't have wasted a second telling him how horrible he was acting. He watched Allison as she stared out the window. A tear rolled down her face. He was ashamed of his callousness.

"Hey."

She waved a hand at him. "I'll be fine. I just want to go home. If I leave town, they'll forget about this and it will be over. I'll be too far away. They won't go to that much trouble tracking me back to Houston. I could be out of here and back home in a few hours. They won't even know I've left."

He wished he could tell her she was right. He'd drive her back to Houston himself if he thought it could work. There was still so much he wasn't allowed to tell her, yet. Like the fact that the dead woman was a DEA agent, and the man in the truck was a cartel member who was a cold-blooded killer. Jackson didn't want her to know that he'd recognized the man from the picture. He was a known drug dealer who had probably been hired by the cartel to kill the agent and dispose of her body. His photo had been put out by the DEA a few months ago. And now that Allison could ID him, Jackson knew there'd been a hit put on Allison's head, too.

Somehow, the cartel would find her. They wouldn't stop until they knew for certain she was dead. It was their way of protecting themselves. Killing to them was like taking out the trash. It had to be done.

What he didn't know was how they were finding Allison. Texas is a big state. Finding her should be like a needle in a haystack, especially at night in the Hill Country.

Jackson's phone vibrated to signal an incoming text. He picked it up and read it. It was from Devon. He'd seen the email. The text read: BRING HER IN ASAP.

He pulled back onto the road and headed toward town.

"Where are we going?" Her voice shook.

"I'm taking you back to the station. Devon said I need to bring you in."

"I don't feel like answering more questions. I hope it doesn't take too long."

"I can't promise anything, but we're going to figure this out as fast as we can. Now that we have a picture, things have changed. We know who we're dealing with…which doesn't make me feel much better, if you want the truth."

He swallowed hard. Touchy-feely things didn't come easy to him, but he needed to apologize before taking her back to the station. There was a good chance after tonight he'd never see her again.

"Listen, I'm sorry for my mood. I'm pretty grumpy lately."

That was a lie. He was exactly who he always was. Who he'd been since the day his family was taken from him. He didn't care about anyone or anything, but he did feel bad about taking his life's tragedy out on her. It wasn't her fault, and she'd been through way too much to have to put up with him tonight.

"I'm not good at the emotional stuff. Seeing you running for your life and constantly being afraid is wearing on me. I don't always know how to find the right words to say."

"I understand, Jackson," she whispered. "And for the record, you're doing a great job."

His heart seized up at the sadness in her voice. The urge to console her overwhelmed him, but the shock from the unfamiliar emotions left him paralyzed. Before he could think about what he was doing, he reached out to put a hand on her arm.

"Hey."

She turned to face him with mascara smeared under her eyes. Fatigue and fear showed in her features. She was beautiful. He would do whatever it took to keep her safe. He couldn't save Hope or his daughter, but he would save Allison.

"I'll stay with you until this is all over. I won't let anything happen to you. I promise."

"I know, and I want to believe you, but I'm terrified right now."

Before he could say anything more to convince her, headlights closed in on them. The oncoming vehicle was less than two hundred yards away and veering toward the side of the highway. Jackson's instincts kicked in and he thrust his foot on the accelerator. He pulled onto the nearest side road to get off the highway. The car whizzed past mere seconds after he turned. Jackson watched in the rearview mirror as the car skidded to a stop, then made a U-turn and headed back toward them.

"Get down!" He pointed toward the floorboard.

"Do you think that's him? What if he's coming back to kill me?" She hurled questions at him as she ducked her head.

"All the way down." He reached over and eased her down with a firm hand. "Don't move."

He floored the accelerator. The engine revved and whined as he sped away. He glanced in the mirror and watched headlights follow them to an unpaved road. A ping sounded against the car. Allison's scream echoed in his ear.

He had to think of a way to get her off the road. Jackson looked around at the houses, trying to get a bearing for where he was. He passed a road sign that read CR223 and realized if he kept going, it would take him to a dead end in more ways than one.

"Can you shoot a gun?"

"No." Her brown eyes were wide with fear.

"Remind me tomorrow to show you how. Right now, you're getting the crash course."

"What if we don't make it until tomorrow?"

"We will. Just stay down."

Jackson glanced in his mirror. Headlights grew closer. He slammed a palm against the steering wheel.

"Hold on." He flipped off his headlights and turned into the nearest driveway. They headed down the long dirt drive and pulled in behind an old wooden barn. He rolled the window down a couple of inches and turned the ignition off, then unbuckled his seat belt. He leaned down and pulled a .38 revolver from his ankle holster.

"Here," he said, grabbing Allison's wrist. "If something happens to me, you'll need to use this."

"I don't think I can." She pulled away from his grip.

"Yes, you can." He tugged her hand toward the gun and forced her to take it. "Aim and squeeze hard. You have five shots."

She shook her head in protest. "I can't do this, Jackson. I don't know how to shoot a gun, and I can't kill anyone."

He ignored her hesitation. He knew that in a life-or-death situation she would pull the trigger. One thing he'd learned about her was that she was not weak. Allison was a lot stronger than she gave herself credit for. He had to trust her.

"Stay here."

"No, please don't leave me," she whispered.

He hesitated at the fear in her voice, but he knew what he had to do. "Don't let them see you."

Jackson climbed out of the car and pulled his service weapon from his hip. He eased around the side of the garage. Headlights flashed past the end of the long driveway, then stopped. His heart pounded as he waited to see what they were going to do.

A car turned into the driveway and parked. Beads of sweat formed on his brow despite the cold night air. He'd gone his entire career without having to kill anyone. Tonight, he had a sick feeling that was about to change.

He reached up to push the button on his radio. He

tilted his head and whispered the words he hoped wouldn't be his last. "Officer requesting backup. Approximately a half mile down County Road 223."

Before he could say anything else, the car door opened. A man carrying an automatic rifle stepped out.

Jackson raised his weapon and aimed.

Allison held her breath, afraid someone in the darkness would hear her.

Was this how she would leave the world? Facing it this way, she realized her life hadn't been all that great up to this point. With no husband and no kids, it was sobering to think about how little she had to leave behind. Somehow, she knew God had better plans for her than to die like this. Had she been too oblivious or disobedient to see them and missed out?

She closed her eyes and squeezed them tight. The weight of the gun in her hand jarred her to her senses. If someone came to the car, could she shoot them? The thought made her stomach roll.

God, please keep me from having to make that choice.

The slam of a door startled her. Her heart pounded in her ears. Jackson was out there somewhere in the dark protecting *her*, a woman he didn't know and didn't seem to want to know. And yet he was willing to put his life on the line to keep her alive.

A male voice boomed through the air. It wasn't Jackson's.

"I don't know where they went! Do you think I would just let them get away?"

Allison gripped the gun tighter in her hand, careful not to put her finger on the trigger. All she could under-

stand was that he'd said something about getting away.
She couldn't see him, but he sounded a lot like the man
who'd shot at her. She had no doubt he would kill her
now if he knew she was yards from him.

"She got away twice, but it doesn't mean she can get
away again. When I find her, I *will* kill her."

The man's voice trailed off like he was walking back
and forth. She strained to make out every word.

"Keep the information coming. If I do not find her,
then we both die. And remember, no one cares who
you work for."

Allison heard a car door slam again. Maybe there
were two of them. How in the world was she going to
defend herself if two men came after her?

The sound of gravel and tires stopped her heart.
Headlights disappeared, and she heard the car drive
slowly away.

She let out the breath she'd been holding. They were
safe. For now.

"Allison, it's me, Jackson. Don't shoot."

Jackson opened the car door. She lay crouched in the
floor of the car, holding the pistol with a shaking hand.

"Why don't you lay the pistol on the seat. Point it
away from me."

When she did, he reached into the car, gently picked
it up, then put it back into his ankle holster. "I'll need
to teach you how to use this the right way."

"No, I won't need to learn. I hate guns. Besides, I'll
be far away from here tomorrow. The farther away I go,
the safer I'll be. I've made my mind up." She stopped
talking when she remembered that she didn't have a car
to drive home. "I'll get an Uber or something. I will

pick up my car later. My boss would come and get me if I called him."

Jackson slammed the door. "You've made up your mind?"

"Yes, I have." She tilted her chin up in defiance. Nothing he could say would make her change it.

He picked up his cell phone and started reading something. "Well, so have I."

"What's that supposed to mean? And why aren't we leaving? Shouldn't we get out of here?"

"We're sitting here to give them a head start. They need to be far enough away so they won't see us when I pull back onto the road."

She hadn't thought about that. "I'd make a terrible cop. I don't think like a criminal."

"That's exactly why you can't do this by yourself. Not everyone is meant to be a cop. Some people are meant to do…whatever it is you do."

She wasn't sure she liked his tone. She had a very prestigious job working for Avery Guerrero. Everyone in Houston knew who he was, and it had earned her respect, as well. "What's that supposed to mean?"

"Nothing. Just making a point. I already told you, you'd be dead before you made it home, so you're not leaving. Tonight should be proof enough."

"I could stay with friends or get a hotel room far from here."

"And again, you'd be dead by morning." His tone went from firm to irritated.

Her own patience was shattered to bits, and she was tired of his curt attitude. "Stop saying that." She fought to keep her voice from shaking. Confrontation wasn't her strength, but when pushed too far, she wouldn't back down.

Jackson ran a hand through his hair, leaving it in a mess that distracted her. He acted as if he hadn't heard a word she'd said until he faced her.

"Let's talk about this. How do you know for sure you'd be safe? You keep saying that, but you don't even know who these people are. You only think you know. Forget everything you've seen in the movies. This is real, Allison. These people are ruthless. They don't care who you are, who you work for, or that you're a kind and beautiful woman."

Had he just called her beautiful? Her stomach fluttered. How could he compliment her right in the middle of a disagreement? Allison struggled to regain her composure.

"What makes you think they'd come looking for me if I left town?"

His green eyes penetrated her. She inched toward the door and stopped when his hand touched her arm. Tingles shot through her body as she stared down at his hand on her.

"Look at me."

She shook her head, unable to deal with his eyes boring into her. Her ability to deny her feelings for him waned.

"Please, Allison. Look at me." His soft voice pleaded.

She raised her gaze to meet his.

"I'm not trying to scare you. I'm good at looking out for people, but I'm not good at looking out for people's emotions. Maybe I was a long time ago." He shrugged a shoulder. "But not anymore. If I say something to you, it's the truth. I don't lie and I don't sugarcoat things.

When I sound harsh or crass, it's because I don't know any other way to say it. And I don't get upset about something unless I care."

She nodded, unable to reply. It wasn't as if she knew much about him, but she felt sure that he didn't show this side to many people. Without thinking, she placed her hand on top of his. He flinched, but he didn't pull away. She stared into his green eyes, hoping he would say something.

Jackson's hand slid from under hers and traced around her knuckles with a finger. A bolt of electricity shot through her as she watched his hand. Without a word, he inched back under the steering wheel and started the car.

Jackson stopped and waited at the end of the long drive for backup to arrive. His heart still raced from touching her hand. It was stupid of him and he knew it. Saving her should be the only thing on his mind. Ever since she'd come into his life, things were upside down. His feelings were all over the place because of this woman. For the past five years, he'd avoided relationships. And for good reason. But avoiding Allison wasn't an option. He needed to keep his mind straight if he wanted to keep her alive. From here on out, he'd force himself to focus on the job.

Fortunately, he'd gotten a good look at the man when he'd stepped out of the car. There was no mistaking that it was the man from her picture. Jackson couldn't hear both sides of the conversation, but what he did understand sent chills down his spine. It was time to call Devon and let him know.

As soon as he heard the call connect, he started talking.

"Hey, I got a good look at the guy."

"Where's the girl? Is she still with you? The DEA needs their witness, Jackson."

"Yeah, yeah, we're fine. Listen to me, they're headed north on County Road 223. I can't protect her alone out here in the dark. They got close, Devon. Too close."

"Is backup there yet?"

"I see them coming up the road now." Jackson kept his eyes on the approaching headlights.

"Let them guide you in. Whoever this is, they won't make a move with cops surrounding her. What I'd like to know is how they found her and how they keep finding her."

"That's what I'd like to know, too. Do you think someone in the department is tipping them off?"

"I don't want to speculate too much right now, Jackson."

Jackson agreed with Devon. He ended the call and rested his forehead on the steering wheel. He'd give anything to have his wife waiting at home for him tonight. He always loved coming in from work to a warm hug. Reality stirred him, bringing him back to his senses.

"Is something wrong?"

For a split second he'd lost himself in the past. He sat up and nodded without saying a word. He didn't want to tell her his next plan, but it was better to get it over with.

"I'm not only bringing you in—I'm putting you in a cell. You're going to jail tonight."

He felt her eyes boring into him and heard her gasp.

"What? Why?"

"Protection. So you won't leave."

"I've never been to jail before. Besides, jail seems harsh considering I'm not the criminal. Why can't I go to the safe house? Wasn't that the plan before they told you to bring me into the station?"

"Yes, and that was also before you kept threatening to leave town by yourself. You're hardheaded, you know. It's not like you'll be treated as a criminal, but I can't let anything happen to you, Allison. Trust me, it won't be as bad as you're thinking."

"You have no idea what I'm thinking."

"Enlighten me." He shot her a half grin.

She cleared her throat. "I think you resent me for getting you into this mess. I think you were planning on ending your shift, then going home to your quiet house and quiet life. Then I came along and messed it all up."

"*This* is all part of my job. I don't resent you."

That was a lie. He did resent her, but not for the reasons she'd just stated. He resented her for making him feel things he wasn't ready to feel. But she didn't need to know that.

She turned away. "I want to go back to Houston. I've done nothing wrong, so you have no legal right to lock me up." She sniffed.

"Don't cry. I hate seeing women cry."

She spun around. Anger flashed behind her brown eyes, causing him to flinch.

"Why? Because you feel responsible? Besides, I'm not crying." She lifted her chin and crossed her arms.

He'd give her points for knowing how to hit a guy where it hurt. "Yes, I'm probably the reason some women have cried, but it was never on purpose."

"Well, I'll have you know that I'm not delicate, but I

will not spend the night in jail, either. Figure out something else."

"There is nothing else that keeps you safe. You're a flight risk. This is the only way."

She exhaled loud enough for him to hear it, then pointed her finger at him. "I'm not spending the night in jail."

A smile tugged at the corner of his mouth. If she was anything, she was feisty. He liked that about her. Sweet as honey until she was backed into a corner. He caught himself as his mind tried to go back to the past. This time, he fought against it.

"What were you grinning at?"

"You. And you might want to keep that finger tucked away before you go pointing it in my face again."

"You're making me nuts. And for the record, I'm not afraid of you."

Afraid? What would she say that for? He wasn't trying to scare her. "Why would you say you're not afraid of me? I'm not trying to throw my weight around with you. I have too much respect for you to do that. I don't treat women that way."

"It feels like you're trying to boss me around a lot and that you don't have much regard for my thoughts and feelings."

"Again, not what I was trying to do." He was getting tired of always saying how sorry he was. "I'm not going to keep apologizing for everything I say. I know I'm grumpy and blunt, but never mistake that for being unsympathetic to your feelings."

Her shoulders slumped in defeat. "I know. I'm not used to running for my life or spending time in hospitals or jails...or dodging bullets or getting poisoned..."

He couldn't help himself and a laugh escaped at her expense.

After a few seconds, she giggled. "I sound so pathetic."

"You're what my nephew calls a hot mess." They both laughed. It felt good to ease the stress with a little silliness.

She put her hands on her hips. "Well, are you gonna save my life or not?"

He smiled at her. "Yes, ma'am. Or I'll die trying."

The laughter faded from her eyes. "Please don't. I've lived through a lot of things but never someone losing their life for mine. I don't think that's something I could get over."

Jackson noticed the headlights coming closer. A sick feeling washed over him. It wasn't a Stonewater cruiser. He shoved her head down. "Get onto the floor."

She did it without asking any questions. The fear in her eyes told him that she knew what was happening. He put the squad car into reverse and backed down the long drive. He remembered being called to a domestic dispute at a residence nearby a few months ago. A woman had driven her car out to the back roads and her husband couldn't find her. Jackson had driven everywhere looking for her. He'd taken a turn down a long road that ended up crossing the creek bed. They needed to find that creek because it was their only hope. Turning on his headlights would give them away, so he did the best he could to maneuver the car using only the moonlight.

Allison bounced around on the floorboards as the car rolled over rocks and holes.

"Why do you think they came back?"

"Someone tipped them off." He slapped the steering wheel. "I wish I knew who the rat was."

"Who could have done that? No one knew we were back here except the police station."

"Exactly."

"Do you think someone in your department is dirty?"

Just the idea of it made his insides recoil. Nothing in this world sickened a cop more than finding out one of your own was corrupt.

"I don't know, but I'm sure someone's telling them where you are."

"Who do we trust?"

"No one."

EIGHT

"Not even your friend, Devon?"

She watched the lines in Jackson's face harden. He didn't say a word. Reading people had never been her strong suit. And this man was especially hard to read. Probably all the years he'd spent as a cop had taught him how to keep a straight face.

"What now?" she asked. She didn't press the issue about his friend.

"Devon is clean. You can trust him. I know where we can hide for the night. Once the sun comes up, we'll head to the station."

After he'd said not to trust anyone? Not on her life. Literally. "Uh-uh. I'm not going there. I was adamant before, and now that you've confirmed there's a dirty cop, there's no way I'm going there."

He hit a bump, and she grimaced as her shoulder hit the underside of the dash. "Can I get up now?"

"Just stay out of sight."

She climbed onto the seat and lay down.

Neither said a word as he drove. The car finally came to a stop, and when he turned off the engine, she could hear water trickling over rocks. "Can I sit up now?"

"Yes, crouch down and stay low."

"Where are we?"

"Stoney Creek. We're parked down at the creek bed. They won't see us down here."

"Are you sure?"

"No, but I'm hoping."

She laughed. "You're always so blatantly honest."

"I thought that was a good quality."

"To someone it probably is, but I'll get used to it."

She regretted the words the second they left her mouth. "But it's a good thing I'll be heading back to Houston as soon as we find the thugs trying to kill me."

"Why don't you try to get some sleep?" He patted the seat.

"Seriously? I can't sleep. There's no way I'll be able to sleep out here. Won't we get cold without the heater?"

"I'll turn on the heat if it gets too cold. There are some blankets in the trunk. I'll get them."

She grabbed his arm as he reached for the door handle. "No. The cab lights will come on. They'll see you."

He looked down at her hand and smiled. "You're starting to think like a cop. Don't worry, I was going to turn them off."

Jackson grabbed two blankets from the trunk. He tossed them to her and climbed back into the car.

"See, quick as lightning." He unfolded a blanket and spread it over her. His hand pulled her long hair aside. The gentle gesture went straight to her heart. She was beginning to understand that his rough exterior was only there to hide his pain. He'd made it clear that his wife and daughter meant everything to him, and without them, his world didn't exist anymore. It didn't take a genius to see through Jackson Archer, but it would take dedication to get to his heart.

"You comfortable now?"

"Yes, thank you." She smiled and settled herself under the blanket.

He braced both hands on the steering wheel and looked straight ahead, his eyebrows furrowed. "I really think we have a dirty cop."

"Should you say something? Isn't there a way to report it?"

"No, I don't have any real proof, other than saying I think it's how these people keep finding you. And that won't hold up when making an accusation like that. It's only a gut feeling."

"Why wouldn't you speak up, anyway?" She wanted to think that if she saw or suspected someone of doing something wrong, she'd do the right thing and tell. But she didn't want to judge him for his decisions.

"It doesn't work like that. We're brothers. I can't go making accusations against one of my brothers. Ever heard the saying, 'I've got your six'?"

She hadn't. Her close circle of friends and family weren't law enforcement. "No, never."

He dragged a hand through his short brown hair, leaving it in a tousled mess. She noticed it was a habit because he did it often. It only made him look more ruggedly handsome. She didn't realize she was staring until he arched his back and tugged at his duty belt. His tight uniform stretched across his muscular chest. She diverted her eyes and silently scolded herself.

"What does it mean?" Her voice quivered. She grimaced, hoping he didn't notice.

He pulled the blanket's edge around her and tucked it behind her shoulder. "You sound like you're shivering."

She smiled. "Thanks." It wasn't the cold that caused her voice to crack. The heat of embarrassment warmed her cheeks.

"I've got your back."

"Huh?"

"The saying. I've got your back. That's what it means."

"Oh, right." She needed to get herself together. She didn't know why she was suddenly feeling nervous around him. He was handsome, especially in his uniform, but this man had more baggage than an airport. He'd made it clear, not in words but in actions, that there would never be another woman as wonderful as his wife.

Not that she didn't understand his feelings. She couldn't imagine what he was going through or had been through. Whatever she was feeling, she would squelch it. She wanted to find a great man one day, but this one was not it.

"Did you say something?"

Her head snapped up. Had she been talking out loud? "What?"

"You seem weird. Is your head hurting? How's the stitches in your knee? Maybe it's the effects of that hit you took. It hasn't been that long since your accident or since they drugged you. I might need to get you to the hospital."

"Honestly, I'm fine." She wasn't about to admit that he was the reason she seemed so weird.

He threw his palms up into the air. "If you say so."

"How long do we need to wait here?"

"I don't know. I sent Devon a message and told him our location. He's trying to find us."

"Do you really trust him?" She had to ask again for her own peace of mind.

"With my life. We go way back. We went to college together, and we were in the police academy together. He was the only one there for me when Hope and Natalie died."

She didn't want to say anything in response. He didn't like talking about his family, so she didn't want to upset him. Especially while they were stranded in the middle of nowhere.

"You remind me of her."

Allison's heart smacked her chest. "Me?"

A grin lifted one corner of his mouth and his eyes lit up. "Yeah, you. Do you see anyone else in this car?"

She smiled. "Thank you, Jackson. I'm sure whatever it is, I can take that as a compliment." Her heart fought to regain its normal rhythm.

Jackson's eyes darkened as he studied her face. His eyes drilled into hers. It wasn't anger that she saw, but something else. Confusion. Maybe even fear. Whatever it was, it faded into another gentle smile.

"You're the kindest person I've met in a long time."

"Thank you. I wish I could say the same, but…"

His laughter filled the car. "Touché."

The ringing of his cell phone broke the mood. He was all business again.

Headlights beamed over the hill and into the creek bed.

"Hey."

In the night's silence, Allison could hear the voice on the other end.

"Those headlights are mine. That's your car down there, right?"

"Yeah, it's us."

He disconnected the call and turned to Allison. "Wait here. It's Devon. I need to talk to him." He turned on the car ignition and switched up the heat. "Stay warm."

He shut the car door and walked around to lean on the trunk. Devon pulled up and climbed out of his unmarked patrol car, rubbing his chin and shaking his head. "I have a bad feeling. This is all making me sick in the stomach."

Jackson had the same revolting impression. It was obvious his friend wasn't telling him something. He knew Devon had been keeping secrets from him since this whole thing started. Way back when they'd found out the identification of the DEA agent in the truck, Devon had been acting aloof. Jackson knew his friend well enough to know when he was being evasive. Since Devon was the detective, it wasn't like he had to tell Jackson everything, but their friendship usually trumped protocol.

"Come on, Devon. What's going on? I've got a woman in my car who's scared to death and running for her life. How do these guys know she's with me? How do they keep finding me? Tell me the truth, man."

"All right. But you're not going to like it."

Jackson stared into Devon's eyes. He sensed more than just bad news.

"We don't have time to stand here talking, Jackson. They want you to bring her in."

"They?"

"FBI. They want her brought in."

Jackson shoved a hand into his hair and spun around. His stomach knotted. He leaned against the car. "Something big is going on."

"Yeah. The DEA and FBI, they're all part of this now. We're on the sidelines watching. I have no idea what's going on or what's going to happen next. They're not telling me much."

Jackson shot him a look. Devon always knew the details about every murder case that went through the department.

"I'm not lying to you. We're getting information on a need-to-know basis. Which I'm assuming we don't need to know, because they aren't talking to us about anything. All I've learned is that the DEA has been on a case here in Stonewater for a while. They're not saying more than that. This is huge, Jackson. Feds are crawling all over our station. That woman in your car woke up a rattlesnake den when she flipped that truck."

"Why the FBI?" Jackson kicked a rock into a tree. "If the agent was DEA, who brought in the FBI? Why not the Texas Rangers?"

"Beats me." Devon shrugged both shoulders.

"Do the feds know she can ID the man in the truck?"

"Yeah, they know. They told us they're taking over the case and we're only here to assist."

Jackson turned and looked through the back window of the cruiser. "What do they know about her? I'm sure they've been digging deep into her background."

"She's got one sister, no kids, no husband. She was engaged once. She works for that Houston restaurant tycoon, Avery Guerrero at Paradigm Enterprises. She's his personal assistant. She's a member of a church in

Houston where she was a Sunday school teacher for a couple years. She adopted two cats from a no-kill animal shelter and has always paid her taxes on time. The perfect girl, if you ask me."

Jackson shot him a look. "Perfect for what?"

Devon raised an eyebrow. "You sure are edgy."

"Yeah, well, she's no good to anyone in a body bag. Let's get her back to the station. We can figure out the rest once we get there."

"There is no *we*, Jackson. As soon as you get her to the station, you're off this case."

Jackson looked back at her through the window. He didn't know why handing her over to the feds bothered him so much. This was his job. He knew the rules. It shouldn't be making him feel like this. "I promised her I wouldn't let anything happen to her."

"And it won't. You're making good on your promise. The DEA will take care of her. Now, let's get her out of here. She can ride with me to the station. We'll try to throw them off as much as we can. The cartel has eyes everywhere, and I don't know who in our department is on their payroll. Probably don't want to know, but I have an idea."

Jackson bristled. "Who are you thinking of?"

He rubbed his chin with a thumb and shook his head. "I don't want to say any names, but someone is tipping them off. Someone at the top. But let me make it clear—it's not the chief."

He knew it wasn't their chief. Jackson had never met a more honest man in his life. But it was somebody. Dealing with a dirty cop was worse than dealing with a criminal. They knew the system and how to play it. The betrayal was close to that of a cheating spouse. The signs were always there, but you just didn't want to believe it because the truth hurt too much.

"All right, Detective. You're calling the shots now. I'll go tell her." Jackson opened the car door. "Hey, time to go. Devon is going to drive you back to the station."

"Why?" Her eyes pleaded with him, sending his insides sliding south.

"Plans have changed a little. We're taking every precaution we can to keep you safe, so we're putting you in a different car."

Her eyes searched his face for answers. He wasn't about to give her any, not yet.

"I want to stay with you, Jackson."

She couldn't have shocked him more if she'd slapped him. His entire body felt a yearning that he'd thought he was no longer capable of. He took in the sight of her looking up at him with soft, pleading eyes. She was giving him her trust, but she was taking his heart in return.

That thought snapped him back to reality. She was trying to lay claim to a heart that was stone cold. And always would be. She was too good for him. Allison Moore deserved better than a jaded cop with an attitude.

"Come out so we can get you to the station." He turned his head, refusing to look at her. He couldn't bear to see the hurt in her eyes. "Devon will take care of you."

As he slammed the car door, he was glad Devon was taking over. The more space he could put between them, the better. He didn't want a woman in his life messing with his head. Or his heart.

Devon stared at him with a scowl on his face.

Jackson bristled. "What is it now?"

"Nothing. I don't even feel like arguing with you." Devon shook his head in obvious disapproval.

"Good, because I can't wait to get home and put this whole mess behind me. The feds can have this case. And her, too."

NINE

Allison picked up her cell phone and let her finger hover over her parents' number. They needed to know what was going on, but would she be putting their lives in danger, too? She shoved her phone back into her purse. Her resolve was crumbling, and she didn't know how much longer she was going to be able to hold it together.

Devon opened the car door and peered inside. "Hey, Ms. Moore. You're coming with me to the station."

Allison nodded and slid out of the car. She walked past Jackson and glanced up at him. Just when she thought she was out of his reach, he laid a gentle hand on her shoulder. She stopped and turned to face him.

"Allison, I promise you'll be safe."

She looked into his green eyes. They were softer than they'd been a few seconds ago, but there was still a coldness in them that told her he was giving her all the compassion he could muster. She knew in her heart that he was a good man who was capable of love once, but now? She honestly didn't know.

"It's a good thing you don't have to worry about me anymore."

He stared at her with the furrowed brow that she'd become accustomed to. Without giving him a chance to reply, she walked around the car and got in, hoping to hide her face from him. Hot tears burned her eyes. She didn't know why it mattered so much to her that he was handing her over to someone else. It wasn't like they meant anything to each other. She knew he was only following orders, but it still hurt that he seemed angry and irritated with her. She closed her eyes, fighting to hide the fresh tears that threatened to spill down her face.

Dear God, I don't always pray for others like I should, but please hear me now. Please protect me... and please heal Jackson Archer from his grief. Amen.

Devon climbed into the car. "He means well."

"Maybe so, but it sure is hard figuring him out. I never know if I've offended him or not."

Devon laughed. "No one does."

"I feel sorry for him."

"Well, don't let him hear you say that. He's got a lot of pride. The last thing Jackson Archer wants is to be pitied. He's had a rough five years, but he's way better now than he was in the beginning."

Allison wondered if focusing on her feelings for Jackson was her way of keeping her mind off someone trying to kill her. She had a bad habit of ignoring the big things and focusing on something irrelevant when things got serious. When dealing with her ex-fiancé, she'd thrown herself into her job, her church and working out. She tried everything from cake-baking lessons to tae kwon do classes, but nothing hid the pain.

What if she cared about Jackson more than she wanted to admit? Even if she did, her sister was right about him having a lot of issues. She wondered what really happened to his family. Something inside her had to know the truth.

"Can you tell me what happened? To his family, I mean?"

"Someone ran them off the road. It was horrific. I still can't believe the driver didn't stop to render aid."

Allison gasped. "It was a hit and run?"

"Yes. No one could identify the car that hit them. No one saw it happen. I've never stopped working the case, but all I've ended up with are more questions."

"Not knowing who killed his family must be agonizing for him."

"I don't even pretend to know what he's gone through. He's a good man, but he's never been one to show his soft side. His dad was an army colonel. Their home was like a mini boot camp. He always told stories about how strict his dad was when they were growing up. Hope brought out a side of him that no one else could. Now that she's gone, he's back to being salty on a daily basis."

"He's definitely that, all right."

"Don't let him get to you. He's a good cop, and he's focused on keeping you safe."

He was a good cop, she knew that much about him, but it sure seemed like he took the first opportunity to get rid of her. So much for his promises.

"Then why'd he let you take me in?"

"My idea."

"Why?"

"He didn't tell you? The DEA and FBI are taking over the case. We were trying to get you to a safe house, but things keep changing on us. I wish I could tell you everything, but there's a lot going on that I can't discuss with you. They pulled us off the case. Now that other agencies are taking over, we're only assisting. We're still going to look out for you, though. We'll protect you, no matter what."

Lights up the road caught her attention. "Devon, are those federal agents?" Allison pointed toward the lights.

Devon threw the car door open and yelled. "Jackson!"

Jackson opened the passenger door of Devon's car and grabbed Allison by the arm. "Come on. We need to get you out of here."

Everything went into fast-forward. Jackson held her hand as they ran toward the creek bed. Devon followed behind them.

The cold air numbed her nose and ears. She winced as the stitches in her knee pulled. Her breath clouded around her as she ran. The familiar ping of something hitting metal echoed through the darkness. "Are they shooting the car?"

"Get down!" Devon yelled. The three of them dove behind a large pile of rocks and tree branches left behind from a recent flood.

"What's happening?" Her voice shook as her teeth chattered against the cold air.

"Just stay down," Jackson said.

"Jackson, what if they find us?"

He grabbed her wrist and pulled her closer. "They won't."

Jackson's heart was heavy as he watched her. He knew Devon could handle himself in any situation, but knowing Allison was in the middle of this was making him uneasy. He wanted to have confidence in her, but even a trained police officer didn't want to be put in a gunfight.

Whatever it was that she'd uncovered, these thugs weren't going to stop until she was either dead or in their possession. And he wasn't going to let either of those happen.

The rapid fire of a gun jolted him. Jackson grabbed Allison and placed a hand over her mouth to stifle the scream he'd anticipated. Bullets hitting metal filled the night air. Their patrol cars were being riddled with holes.

Allison trembled under his arms. He put a finger up to his lips to signal her to be quiet. He knew it was hard for her to stay calm because his own heart pounded in his chest like a drum.

"Jackson, take her. I'm going to see if I can get a look at their faces. We need to figure out who these people are. Radio for backup and get her to safety."

"Devon, no," she whispered. "You can't stay here. What if they find you?"

Devon ignored her and kept his focus on Jackson. "Richard Maber has a place about a mile up the hill. He's out of town. He asked me to feed his cat for him while he's gone. There's a key under the rock by the front door."

"The only way to that hill is through the creek." Allison shook her head in disagreement.

"Right." Devon patted her on the back. "You can do it."

Jackson frowned at the suggestion. He wasn't worried about himself, but he couldn't put Allison into another life-threatening situation. "It's got to be close to freezing out here again tonight."

"If y'all have a better idea, let's hear it. Otherwise, get moving. It's only a matter of minutes before they realize we're not in those cars."

Jackson grabbed Devon's shoulder. "Meet us there when the coast is clear."

"I will. Now get moving."

Jackson bent down and pulled his backup revolver from his ankle holster. "Here." He thrust his gun into her hand. "Carry this for me." He pulled his service pistol from its holster and tucked it under the shoulder of his bulletproof vest. The last thing he needed was a waterlogged gun.

Allison stared down at the weapon.

Without saying a word, Jackson took it from her hand and emptied the chambers. He dumped the bullets into his pocket, then handed it back.

Without waiting for her to reply, Jackson grabbed Allison's hand and pulled her toward the water. Parts of the creek were shallow, but after the recent flooding, the water was still a little higher than usual. He hoped he could find a place to cross that wasn't over her head.

"Can you swim?"

"Yes, but..."

He didn't give her time to finish. Grabbing her hand, he led her to the frigid water. "Try not to get your arms and head in the water. Keep as much of your body dry as you possibly can."

"Okay," she said, her voice no more than a whisper.

He knew it terrified her. As much as he tried to hide it, he was as scared as she was. Not for himself, but for her.

"Walk slowly." He stepped in first. "You're going to suck in a deep breath when your chest hits the cold water. Cover your mouth if you think you'll make a noise. We don't want them to hear us."

She followed him biting her lip as she anticipated the jolt of the frigid water.

Jackson braved the shock of the cold creek as it surrounded him. His boots filled up, making his steps heavier. The water temperature was close to freezing even though he didn't see any ice. He eased his feet across the slick rocks as he anticipated a sudden drop off.

Memories of swimming in this same creek with Hope and her friends flashed in his mind. He was familiar with the creek's different depths. He knew parts of it were shallow enough to walk through, but the darkness made it too hard to tell whether or not they'd found a good crossing.

Jackson glanced back at her and noticed the anguish in her face. The cold was painful, and he worried she wouldn't make it across.

In the shadows, he could make out the tree line less than forty yards ahead. The water was only at his waist and he hoped it stayed that way. Jackson felt Allison's hand grip his tighter.

"Hang in there. Do you think you can make it a few more minutes?" He fought to get the words out. The freezing air in his lungs tightened his chest. His teeth chattered, cutting off any words he wanted to say.

"Y-y-yes," she stuttered.

Her arm drooped and she struggled to hold it up. Jackson pulled her hand into the air to keep it from falling into the water.

"You're doing great. We're almost there."

When they made it more than halfway across, he felt a sense of relief. Jackson took another small step to feel for the rocks beneath his boot. His next step plunged him deeper, putting him in chest-deep water. Panic set in as he sucked in a sharp breath. Allison was at least six inches shorter. He couldn't let her go under.

"H-hold on." The cold was taking over his body. Jackson turned around and put his back to her. "Get on." He bent slightly to allow her to get a good grip on him. She struggled to pull herself up. He reached into the bitter cold water and pulled her legs up to his side. Her arms wrapped around his neck as her breath tickled his cheek.

A few more feet to go and they would be out of the creek. Jackson fought the last few steps of the freezing current until the water began draining away from his body. Once he had her on the dry bank, he let her slide down from his back.

"Come on. We need to keep moving. Are you all right?"

"So cold," she whispered.

"I know. The house is right up this hill."

Gunfire erupted into the darkness, sending them scrambling up the embankment.

Jackson could only hope that his friend had found cover. He longed to turn around and rush back to Devon, but he had to help Allison. He grabbed her hand and squeezed as her fingers wrapped around his. Shots rang out as they ran up the hill. He argued with himself about leaving her to help Devon, but as they ran, he knew there was only one choice to make. Devon was trained for these situations. Allison wasn't.

"Come on," he said, pulling her with him.

TEN

Allison followed Jackson up the steep hill holding on to his hand for dear life. Just when she thought she couldn't walk another step, she noticed lights from a nearby house.

"It's right up here." Jackson's steps quickened.

"Will we be safe?"

"I won't let you out of my sight." He squeezed her hand and pulled her in step with his pace.

Allison pulled away and turned to face him. "How do you know we'll be safe here? They're right down there. With guns."

Ignoring her questions, he tugged her hand. "Come on. We don't have time to stand here. I have to get you warm."

They reached the house, and she watched as he pulled a key from under a rock. He unlocked the door with a shaking hand. A blast of warmth blanketed them as he opened the front door. The golden glow of a small lamp shone on his face. His hair was in a spiky mess, but he'd somehow managed to keep it dry.

"Come on. We have to find you some warm clothes and a blanket."

Relief steadied her breathing. Her body still trembled from a mixture of the frigid water and fear.

"I feel like we're breaking in."

"We are. Come this way."

Allison followed him. His wet boots squeaked against the linoleum floor. He pushed a door open and flipped on a light. He reached down and pulled the ends of her wet hair from her collar. His cold fingers brushed her neck, sending new shivers down her body.

"You need to hurry and get those clothes off and dry your hair. See if you can find a hair dryer. I'll go look for some clothes for you to wear."

He shut the door and reappeared a few minutes later, tapping on it.

"Hey, I have something for you."

Allison stood behind the door as she opened it. She stuck her hand out to retrieve what he'd found. "Thank you. You should change into something dry, too." She shut the door and examined the clothes.

"I don't think that's going to happen. Hurry up. I'm going to light a fire so we can warm up a little."

Allison emerged wearing a pair of women's sweat-pants that were a couple of inches too short and a large bulky sweater that fell just above her knees.

She caught him bent over tending to a blazing fire. His wet boots were propped against the hearth to dry. He was wrapped in a blanket, barefoot and still wearing his wet uniform. Jackson looked up from the fire-place and grinned. "You're definitely safe here. They'll never find you in that sweater."

Allison looked down and giggled. She immediately felt guilty for taking the time to laugh while Devon was still out there.

"What about Devon?"

"He'll be all right. Devon isn't going to stay there and put himself in danger."

"I hope you're right."

A look of concern flashed over his face. He was worried, too. If something happened to either of the two men, she'd never forgive herself for bringing them into this situation.

"Please don't hide things from me to protect me. I can take the truth. Do you think they will ever give up trying to find me?"

"I know if any woman can handle the truth, it's you."

"What's really going on? It's only been a couple of days since that truck ran me off the road, and look at everything that's happened to me. You're a cop. Can't you make any sense of this? What would make them want to kill me? Just because I stopped to help?"

He shot her a look that said he didn't want to talk about it.

"At least tell me what you're thinking."

He turned to face her. "Allison, I don't know what to think. You've been shot at and drugged. You can ID the man who was transporting the body of a murdered DEA agent. Right now, I don't know much more than you do. I'm only trying to keep you alive."

"How long can we stay here?"

"I don't know. But for now it's all I've got and you have to warm up."

"So do you."

"I'm fine." He turned to face the fireplace and held out his hands.

"Aren't you cold in those wet clothes?"

"No." His short, curt tone made her flinch.

Allison fought the urge to snap back at him. Instead, she sat on the floor next to where he stood and held her feet up to the fireplace. The warmth soothed her ragged nerves.

"Your hair is still wet." His tone had simmered down but she could still hear the edge in it.

"I couldn't find a hair dryer. Why haven't you changed clothes?"

He laughed. "You don't know Richard Maber. He's about your size. There's nothing in this house that would fit me. That sweater is the biggest thing in the house."

"Oh." Heat crept from her neck to her cheeks, and it wasn't because of the fire. "Jackson, I feel horrible."

"For what?"

"Getting you involved in this. Getting Devon involved in this."

"This is my job. It's Devon's job, too. You didn't get me involved. I told you—I do this for a living."

"You help women run for their lives for a living?"

Jackson grinned. "Not exactly, but you know what I mean."

"What if you can't save me? What if something bad happens?"

His brow creased. He rammed a metal poker at a glowing log.

"I couldn't live with myself if something happened to you…or Devon."

Jackson poked harder at the log until it broke into two pieces. "Just because I couldn't save my wife doesn't mean I can't save you."

Allison inhaled a sharp breath. His words hit her like a sucker punch. "I didn't mean it like that, Jackson."

He dropped the poker and pulled both palms down his face, then sat on the floor next to her. She stayed quiet for fear of upsetting him more.

Jackson turned to face her. He lifted her chin with a finger and allowed his gaze to move from her mouth to her eyes. "It's okay. I'm stressed out and taking it out on you."

Although she was drying out, her body shivered against her will. Jackson took the blanket from around his shoulders and draped it over hers. Words escaped her as she stared at him. Jackson Archer was a gorgeous man. Inside and out.

He tucked the blanket around her and pulled her into him. The smell of his cologne still lingered on his skin. She closed her eyes and listened to the sound of his breathing. She lost herself in the moment until his voice startled her.

"I don't mean to be rough and callous with you. It's just that… I'm not good at having a soft side."

"Yes, you are, Jackson. I know it's in there. I've seen it. I'm seeing it right now."

"Hope always brought it out in me. No one else since her, though. Not until you." He rubbed her arms through the thick blanket. "I've only known you a few days, but you remind me so much of her."

Allison's heart sank. No matter how much she tried to tell herself that she didn't care for him, the truth was that she did. He didn't seem to be ready for a relationship. Even if they tried, would he always compare her to his wife? She couldn't measure up to someone who meant the world to him. She could never be Hope.

For now, she wouldn't think about it. She only wanted to enjoy the moment. She snuggled closer to him and sighed. His wife had been a blessed woman. Deep down, all Allison ever wanted was to be that important to someone.

But Jackson Archer had already found that person.

A rap sounded on the front door. Jackson spun around and grabbed for the gun lying beside him on the floor. A man stepped inside before he could draw his weapon.

"Y'all okay in here?" Devon slammed the door and stood shivering as water dripped from his clothes.

"Man, what is wrong with you?" Jackson set the gun back on the floor next to him and exhaled. "I could've shot you."

"You really think the cartel knocks?"

He heard Allison stifle a giggle. "What about our squad cars?" Jackson stood up and walked to the door.

"We're not going to be driving those again."

"Great. We're sitting ducks here."

"Richard has a pickup in the garage. We'll take that."

Allison watched the two men exchange a worried look.

"What about Allison?"

Devon cocked an eyebrow at him. "Well, we have to get her to the station and hand her over to the feds. Remember? Or did the cold freeze your brain?"

Jackson shook his head. Devon's witty comebacks were growing old. He reached for his boots and began to put them on. He wasn't about to turn Allison over to anyone. Not until they knew whom to trust.

"No, we're not."

"What do you mean? We don't have a choice. Think about this, Jackson," Devon pleaded with him.

"Not yet. Not until we can figure this out. We have a rat, Devon. You and I both know it. Somebody is tipping these people off. How can I guarantee her safety if I turn her over to them?"

"Then we'll take her to your house. You can keep an eye on her until I can figure something out. She'll be safe there as long as we don't tell anyone where we are."

Allison stood up and walked toward them. "What if they find me at your house?"

"No, that won't happen." Devon shook his head adamantly. "No one will know you're there. Only the three of us."

"How can you be sure of that?" Allison looked at both men.

"We can't." Jackson stared at the ground. He wanted to lie and tell her they had this all figured out, but they didn't.

"Okay then, let's go." Devon led them to the garage, where they climbed into a crew cab, four-wheel-drive pickup truck.

Allison started to climb into the front seat, but Jackson stopped her. "No, get into the back." He saw a hurt look cross her face. "Lay down so no one knows you're in here."

"Oh. I didn't think of that."

Jackson smiled and winked down at her. "That's why I'm here."

"And I'm just along for the ride," Devon quipped. "Get in. We need to move."

They rode to Jackson's place in silence. It was a much-needed break from the reality they were in. He glanced toward the back seat and saw Allison sleeping.

"She's tough." Devon grinned as he looked at her in the rearview mirror.

"Yeah."

"What's going on with you two?" Devon whispered.

"Shh. Cut it out." He wasn't ready to explain anything to Devon or anyone else. The truth was he didn't know what was going on with them. He just knew it was something.

When they reached his house, Jackson opened the truck door to let Allison out. "Here it is. I'll go turn down your bed in the guest room so you can get right back to sleep."

She sat up and yawned but didn't move to get out. "Hey, you can get out now."

Tears filled her eyes as she stared straight ahead. She didn't have to explain that she'd woken up and realized the nightmare was real. He took her hand and led her out of the vehicle. She followed a bit too close behind him, accidentally stepping on the back of his boot a couple times.

Devon waved, then headed back to the station. He'd promised to call with any new information. Jackson punched in a code on the keypad to unlock the front door. He led her through the foyer and into the living room. He and Hope had designed the house themselves. She'd spent countless hours of decorating to reflect both their tastes. Most people described it as having a rustic charm. He never knew what that meant, but it always seemed to make her happy since that's what she was going for. To him, it was home.

"Your house is amazing."

"Thanks." He motioned toward a staircase at the back of the living room. "Your room is upstairs."

She walked ahead of him as he followed. At the landing, he pointed to the last bedroom on the left. "There's a guest bathroom that connects to the room. You'll have your privacy up here. I'll be sleeping downstairs."

He opened the door and flipped on the light. The bedroom was still decorated the way Hope had left it. White curtains hung over the windows, and a white comforter with a light blue crocheted afghan covered the bed. His mom had made it for them when they'd gotten engaged.

"The sheets should be fresh. The housekeeper comes once a week and changes all the linens. I tried to tell her no one is ever going to stay in this house, but she insists. I'm sure she'll be glad to know someone finally did."

"It's beautiful."

"Again, not my doing. There's a remote for the TV if you feel like watching anything…but on second thought, maybe you should get some sleep."

"Thank you, Jackson. For everything."

Her brown eyes stared up at him. He fought the urge to pull her close and kiss her until all her fears went away. Jackson cleared his throat. "Let me now if you need anything. There's an intercom by the light switch. Just push the button to talk into it. I'll hear it downstairs."

"Your house is fancy…for lack of a better word."

"Hope had a lot of money, if that's what you're getting at."

"No, I wasn't getting at that. I was making an observation."

He shrugged. "She had more than we could ever spend. Her dad designed a computer program for NASA. I couldn't tell you what it did other than make him a lot of money. He died the year after we got married and left Hope a sizable inheritance."

He realized he was rambling, which wasn't something he was used to doing. "Anyway, yell if you need me. Good night, Allison."

He shut the door and inhaled a long, deep breath. What in the world was this woman doing to him? Without warning, guilt settled over him.

This was Hope's home. How could he have thoughts of another woman in this house? Anger swelled in the pit of his stomach. The last thing he would ever do is dishonor the memory of his wife in her own house.

Jackson stormed into his bedroom to change into some dry clothes. He came out and went downstairs to plop into his brown leather recliner. He needed to report his whereabouts and let the captain know about the cars. Although he was off duty now, not reporting in meant he'd be breaking protocol.

It wasn't as if Rusty Schmille would have any sympathy for him. His only hope was to plead his case to the chief when he went back in a few days. The chief was a good man, unlike Schmille. He didn't understand why they kept him around, but like it or not, Jackson had to report to him.

After he punched in the number to the station, he put his feet up and leaned back in the chair. He waited for the captain to answer.

"Schmille."

"Hey, Captain. It's Archer."

"Where have you been, Archer?"

"What do you mean? Devon and I have been calling into dispatch all night. They've had my location."

He gritted his teeth to keep from letting the man know how he really felt.

"The feds are crawling on us over here. This is their case now, and you're running around with their witness. Tell me where you're at and I'll come get her myself."

Something in his gut told him this scenario wasn't right, but nothing about this case was normal.

"No, she needs to rest for the night. She's safe, and I'm not moving her. She's a witness, not a criminal. I can keep her safe until morning."

"Archer, I've got the chief breathing down my neck. I've got feds all over the place. I don't think you're in any position to tell me no. I'm going to ask you one more time. Where is she?"

Jackson's instincts told him to lie, but his training and commitment to the job forced him to tell the truth. Devon was right. They couldn't keep running with her and still uphold the law.

"She's somewhere safe. Sleeping."

"You're joking."

"No."

"Un-stinking-believable. Fine. You'd just better make sure nothing happens to her, Archer. She's their only witness against the cartel. Get her here ASAP."

"After she gets a little rest, sir."

"Archer…be ready to explain to the chief why you broke protocol and didn't bring her in like you were told. I'm not covering for you. You're on your own."

It was a mistake reporting in. Had he known this was going to happen, he wouldn't have made the call.

"What else is new?" Jackson regretted his words as soon as they were out of his mouth. He didn't especially like Rusty Schmille's leadership, but it wasn't like Jackson to be crass with a superior.

"What's that, Archer?"

"Nothing, sir. We'll be in first thing in the morning."

He hung up without letting the captain reply. There was something about Schmille that had always made Jackson leery of the man. There was an abrasiveness to the captain that he'd never grown accustomed to.

Jackson set his phone down on the table and propped his hands behind his head. Sleep would feel good. He hadn't had much of it over the past few days. But real rest would have to wait until he got Allison to the station.

He closed his eyes and fought to ignore the fact that a woman was in his house.

Allison's eyes popped open. Her heart slammed against her chest. Had she heard something? Jackson's house was like a fortress, and there weren't any neighbors around for at least a mile. It was probably a bad dream or something. She lay still as she gave her heart a chance to settle back into a normal rhythm. It must have been a bad dream.

Speaking of bad dreams, right now her life was a living nightmare. Now that she was wide-awake, she fought to push back the reality of what was happening.

She closed her eyes and tried to pray, but a sob lodged in her throat. This wasn't a time to be vulnerable or to melt down. Praying to God meant baring her soul and letting it all out. She hoped He understood, but right now, she couldn't even talk to God about the things that were happening without falling apart. She whispered a short prayer. "You know what's on my heart, Lord. Please keep me safe and let this end soon."

A noise quieted her before she could finish. A thud on the outside wall near the bedroom window echoed through the room.

Allison bolted up. This wasn't her imagination. She waited to hear it again. The silence frightened her as much as the noise had. Maybe Jackson had heard it, too. She fought to steady her breathing and reached for her phone with a trembling hand. She realized she didn't have his number. *Come on, Allison. It's nothing.*

She lay back down and closed her eyes as sleep overcame her again.

A hand closed over her mouth. She tried to scream, but the force on her face was too tight. This time, she wasn't dreaming. She kicked and clawed at the attacker. Where was Jackson? Allison ached to call out to him for help. The hand covering her mouth slipped and she took her chance to yell his name. As soon as his name passed her lips, pain seared through her head. Her body felt limp, and then her world went dark.

Jackson was on his feet holding his pistol before he was sure of what was happening. Something had awakened him. He thought he had heard a noise, but he couldn't be sure if he'd dreamed it or not. He ran to the stairs with his gun drawn. As he passed the foyer, he glanced at the front door. It was shut and locked.

Jackson raced up the stairs and threw open each bedroom door as he passed. He flicked the light on in Natalie's room. Pink and white blinded him as he looked inside. It was the first time he'd opened the door in three years. His legs buckled, and he fought to remain standing. Unbearable pain shattered his heart at the sight of the large dollhouse and the gigantic stuffed white bear sitting next to it.

He slammed the door and moved on. His hand trembled as he reached out to open the next bedroom door. Jackson threw it open and flipped on the light. It was the first time he'd been in there since before the accident. Baby-blue walls and a sports-themed rug lying in front of a crib reminded him of even more that he'd lost. The name "Jacob" hung over the changing table. A shopping bag with brand-new baby items sat in the rocking chair. Never to be used.

Tears burned his eyes. He fought to keep his composure as he scanned the room. Confident no one was in there, he turned off the light and shut the door. He'd never go in there again.

Allison's door was last. So far it appeared that no one had been inside the house. After all she'd been through, he hated to wake her up. She needed her rest. Still, he had to check on her to put his mind at ease. He opened the door without making a sound and peered inside. The last thing he wanted to do was frighten her.

"Allison," he whispered.

Something caught his eye across the room. He pointed his gun toward the window. The shadow moved again in the darkness. He inched closer to the bed where Allison lay sleeping. If someone was behind the curtain, they were as good as dead.

He didn't want to startle her, but he needed her to wake up. Jackson felt the bed. His hand searched for the feel of her leg as he inched it farther up the bed. Nothing. He walked to the window. A cold breeze seeped around the flapping fabric of the curtain.

She was gone.

Jackson flipped on the light to reveal an empty bed. He threw the blankets back to search for any signs of a struggle. Small drops of blood dotted the sheets. A sick feeling washed over him.

He'd failed her.

Just like he'd failed his own family.

Jackson checked all the doors in the house to see how they'd escaped with Allison. After looking in his own room, it was obvious they had entered through the balcony in the master bedroom on the other side of the house. Hope had insisted on installing a set of stairs leading up to it because her home had burned down when she was ten. She'd almost been caught in the fire. He'd conceded because of her fears, even though he didn't like the idea of having outside access to their bedroom.

He always made sure the balcony doors stayed locked. Regardless of the excuses, Allison was still gone. He'd never forgive himself if something happened to her.

Even though guilt was no stranger to him, for once in his life he wished he could actually save someone.

One way or another, he would find her.

ELEVEN

The bag on her head smelled horrid. She wiggled her jaw to loosen the rag from her mouth, but it wouldn't budge. Nausea gripped her. She swallowed hard to fight it back down. She had to stay calm. If she wanted to make it out of this alive, she was going to have to forget about being afraid. She thought of Jackson. Had he even realized she was missing?

How had they gotten past him? Her mind raced to find answers, but nothing made sense. She struggled to kick her feet and move her arms. Whoever had grabbed her in the darkness hadn't walked away unscathed. She'd punched as hard as she could when the bag had been shoved over her head. The blow she received in return had knocked her unconscious. Two hits to the head in the past few days couldn't be good. She wondered how much longer she could keep this up.

The zip ties on her wrists were cutting into her skin, but the ones on her ankles felt loose enough to wriggle out of. She felt around blindly to see if there was anything next to her on the seat. She didn't know if anyone was watching her or even where she was at. If she broke loose, would the consequences be worse?

"What are we going to do with her?"

Allison stilled. She forced her breathing to stop as she listened to the voices. The second voice had a thick Hispanic accent, but she could easily understand him. The first guy was definitely from Texas. His thick drawl was familiar, but his voice wasn't.

"We don't have orders to do anything with her. We have to wait."

"That's loco. We should be able to do whatever we want, and then kill her. I'm hungry, Tex. Can't we stop to eat?

Allison fought to keep a whimper from escaping.

"Calderón hasn't told us what to do yet! You'll follow directions, or else you'll end up dead, too."

"Whatever, man. This is nuts. We kidnapped her like he told us to. We should be able to eat now. Besides, it's not like Calderón will know."

"You're crazy, amigo. You know that?" Tex was clearly agitated with his friend.

Allison heard the other man mumble something in Spanish. She'd learned a little of the language from working with Avery, but she couldn't decipher anything from what he'd said.

"What's that, tough guy? You're gonna kill me, too?" Obviously, Tex understood.

The other man's laugh echoed around her. She guessed they were in a big truck, maybe an eighteen-wheeler. The bumps and jars didn't feel like an average vehicle.

Allison heard the distinct click of a bullet being chambered into a pistol. A sound she hadn't known until this week but knew all too well now. A chill ran down her back. If they were going to kill her, at least she wouldn't know it was coming. She could only pray it would be fast and that it would only take one shot. It would be better if she never knew what hit her.

"Hilarious," Tex said.

Laughter filled the truck. "Sorry, Tex. I've always been told I have a strange sense of humor, amigo, but you might want to get that gun out of my face before I show you how strange my temper can be."

"Let's see how funny you are when you're six feet under the ground like that lady cop. Wasn't that you who did that? You killed her?"

"Guilty," the man replied, his tone smug and icy.

Tears sprang into her eyes. How could she have missed it? It was the man from the truck! She had to get out of there. But how? Only God could help her now. She called out to him with every fiber in her body.

Dear God, I still have so many things left to do in this life. I'm not ready for this. I need Your help to get out of here. If they catch me, please make it quick. Don't let them torture me or leave me in pain. Amen.

She didn't know how her prayer turned from asking to live to begging for a painless death. Whatever happened to her now was completely out of her control. God was all she had in this moment. God was all she'd ever had to get her through life, and she knew He was with her now.

She thought about Jackson and how he was filled with so much anger and grief. She thought about Maddie, her nieces and her parents. How would they handle this? Now wasn't the time to be thinking this way. It was time to fight for her life. As futile as it may be, she had to try. She listened again to the deranged men and their evil conversations. They were still arguing.

"One thing you need to get straight, uh…mee…go, is I ain't scared of you. I could kill you right now."

His drawl was exaggerated and seemed fake. If she had to guess, he wasn't the smarter of the two or the most dangerous.

The truck slowed to a stop, and they both got out without saying another word. This was her chance. She tried to stand but lost her balance. She had to get her bearings, or this wouldn't work. She sat back down to allow the dizziness to pass, but she knew she had to hurry.

This time she slid off the seat and landed on her knees. She bent over. In a quick movement, using all the strength she could muster, she banged her hands against her lower back.

Nothing happened.

It had worked like a charm in her self-defense class. She inhaled a deep breath from inside the dirty bag, forcing herself to ignore the stench. Again, she raised her hands as high as she could behind her back. Her hands smashed down against her body.

The zip tie broke free.

She hurried to remove the bag from her head and pulled the nasty rag from her mouth. She looked around. Her instincts had been right. She was in the sleeper of an eighteen-wheeler. Florescent lights illuminated the small space. Guns were piled around her feet. Pistols, assault rifles, shotguns and boxes of ammunition lay scattered across the floorboard.

A banging noise came from behind the truck. Allison quickly put the bag on her head, placed her hands behind her back and listened. After a few seconds had passed, she felt convinced they weren't getting back into the truck yet. She took the bag off.

There had to be something around the truck that she could use to cut the zip ties off her feet. Since she wasn't wearing shoes, the shoestring trick she'd learned in her self-defense classes wouldn't work.

Fast-food trash lay scattered around her. The stench was revolting. She pushed some garbage out of the way and scanned the floorboard for something to use, taking care not to touch the guns. She spotted a piece of wire sticking out from under the seat of the truck. After a few yanks, it broke.

Allison looped the wire under the zip tie and frantically pulled it back and forth until the plastic snapped.

She was free.

The only thing left to do now was get out of the truck before getting caught. She was glad to see the front seat was cleaner than the back seat, which gave her an easier path to escape. Allison climbed over the custom-made wooden console and plopped down behind the steering wheel. The keys were hanging from the ignition. There was the proof that not all criminals were smart.

She took the keys and shoved them into the pocket of her sweatpants, then picked up a handgun from the back seat. Her hand trembled as she stared at it. *Just pull the trigger.* Jackson's words echoed in her head. Could she really shoot someone? Allison released the clip the way Jackson had done it. It bounced off her leg and landed onto the console with a *thwack*. She snatched it up and popped it back into the gun. At least it was full. She slid the weapon into the band of her sweatpants, then rolled the waistband down a few times to make a pocket, hoping it wouldn't fall out.

She reached to open the door and stopped. Opening the door meant the cab light would come on and they would see her. There had to be a way to turn it off. The dashboard of the big semi was covered with more gadgets and buttons than she had time to study. Time was running out. She had to get out of there. Her mind raced to figure out an escape plan.

Allison noticed the driver's window cracked, so she rolled it down the rest of the way. Her head ached and her wrists stung where the zip ties had cut her, but she ignored the pain. She hoisted a leg out of the window and slid down the door, praying no one would see her. As soon as her feet touched the ground, she heard them.

"Hey!"

Allison didn't wait to see who had yelled at her. She bolted from the truck, racing across the parking lot. Rocks cut into her feet and the stitches in her knee burned with every step.

More yelling came from behind her. Without thinking, she yanked the gun from her waistband and headed for a grove of trees behind the store. Footsteps grew louder. Angry male voices yelled profanity at her as they drew closer. She would never make it to the trees. Allison spotted a couple of green trash dumpsters behind the store. She raced behind them and leaned against one, sucking in gasps of air to steady her breathing. Allison stared down at the gun in her hand.

Just pull the trigger.

Heavy footsteps vibrated the ground. She lifted the gun, pulled the slide back and aimed. He emerged from the shadows, and they locked eyes. Nausea gripped her stomach as she stared at him. She noticed the same beard, same greasy ponytail and same deep wrinkles in his face she'd seen that night on the highway. It was the second time in the past few days she'd encountered him.

He slowly raised both hands into the air, still holding his gun.

Staring at the gun in her own hand, she told herself she didn't have a choice. He'd already tried to kill her once. She knew he was going to follow through if she didn't shoot first. Tears filled her eyes.

"Don't shoot her!"

Footsteps and shouting jarred her back to reality. Allison turned and bolted toward the trees in the distance. Her feet screamed with pain as she flew across large white rocks.

"Stop!"

She zigzagged her way through the skinny mesquite trees. Her foot landed on a sharp stone causing her knees to buckle from the pain.

"Stop running!"

Allison stifled a cry and fought to stand up. Moonlight allowed her to see that she was bleeding.

"I'm not going to hurt you!"

There was that same slow drawl. It was Tex. Did he only want to kill her himself? Is that why he'd stopped the other man?

Fear moved her as she continued to lose distance between them. If he came any closer, she'd have to find the courage to protect herself. Shooting a man wasn't something she wanted to think about, but dying wasn't, either.

Allison limped over a bed of rocks and hid behind a mound of low-growing cactus. She couldn't go any farther. Her feet were bleeding and sore. One more step would be one too many.

The sound of Tex's voice grew louder. "I'm not going to hurt you."

Was he really that dumb? Allison lifted her weapon and braced her soul for what was about to happen.

Tex turned around to scan the woods for any sight of her. He aimed a flashlight at the ground, then bent over to take a closer look. His head popped up and he focused on the woods where she hid. "Come on out. I can see you're hurt and bleeding."

Allison's hand shook as she kept the gun aimed at him.

He stood up. "Come on, ma'am. I promise I won't hurt you. I'm not who you think I am." He started walking toward her. Either he thought she was the stupid one, or he was as dumb as he sounded. Her heart pounded in her ears. A few more steps and he'd be able to reach out and grab her. Her hand trembled under the weight of the gun. She aimed at the treetops above his head and fired.

Tex pulled a weapon from his side and aimed it at her. Allison turned and ran. Without looking back, she went as far as she could until her bleeding feet forbid her to take another step.

She ran until she was certain she couldn't hear anyone behind her. Allison sat on a large rock to nurse the cuts. The temperature was freezing again but at least it wasn't sleeting.

She gazed up at the sky to see the sun peeking over the horizon. The approaching dawn gave her a sense of hope. Asking why this was happening to her was a moot point. She no longer cared why. All she knew was God had carried her this far and He'd take care of her now.

If only she had a cell phone or some way of getting

in touch with Jackson. He'd know what to do. Tears burned her eyes. What if they found her before Jackson did?

The night began to lift from around her as the sun peeked over the horizon. She wondered if Jackson would check in on her this morning and find her empty bed. If only she knew his phone number. She didn't want to call the police department because she didn't know whom she could trust. Calling her family might mean putting their lives in danger, as well. Allison squeezed her eyes tightly and forced herself to calm down. Her mind began to wander. She didn't want to think about what she'd done.

Over the past few years, she'd been through a lot. Having gone through those things made her the strong woman she was today, but in some ways, it also made her weaker. She never knew when the old feelings of worthlessness would creep in. The feeling of not being loved or cared about was a hard memory to shake. Those old feelings of self-doubt were crippling. Clint Mackinaw had ripped her heart out by cheating on her with her best friend. The final blow came when he'd told her she was a horrible girlfriend. He'd also called her ugly and said he couldn't stand the thought of spending his life with a Goody Two-shoes. By his definition that meant anyone who went to church every Sunday.

There'd been signs all along that he wasn't the one for her. Red flags were flying everywhere, but she'd always given him the benefit of the doubt. She knew she was better off without him, but it was hard letting go. After Clint, she'd resigned herself to a life of being single, and for a while she'd enjoyed it.

Allison opened her eyes. Of all the stinking times to start looking back at her pathetic past. She thought about Jackson. He was a good man whether he believed that or not. If she could only call him or reach out to him. Although she'd only known him for a few days, she knew in her heart that he was going to come for her.

The ringing of his cell phone jarred him.

"It's Archer."

Expletives filled his ear. It was Rusty Schmille.

"Sir, slow down. I can't understand a word you're saying."

The man spoke slower in a mocking tone. "Where. Is. She?"

Jackson's stomach knotted. How could he know already?

"She's gone."

"I assume you know what she did?"

Relief washed over him. At least she was alive, but Jackson bristled at the man's tone. "No, sir, I don't know."

"She robbed two men outside of a convenience store. Surveillance caught her running away with a gun in her hand."

Jackson's heart sank. What could've happened to her? And where had she gotten a gun?

Schmille continued his rant. "And you want to know what else? The feds are saying she's with the cartel. You know what I think, Archer? I think they're right. I think she's working with the cartel. Know what else I think?"

He didn't give Jackson time to answer before continuing his tirade.

"I think you've been helping her all along."

"She's not working with the cartel, sir. And if she was, I wouldn't be helping her. I don't think she knows what she's gotten into." His temper started running hot. Allison wasn't working with the cartel. The fact that Schmille was putting that in people's heads was causing Jackson to lose his composure. Not to mention the ignorant accusation that he was helping her. Against his better judgment, he gave in to his anger.

"Every single time I've tried to get her back to the station, something has happened to her. She's been poisoned and shot at. How about you tell me what's going on? All you care to do is sit in your office and shout orders and obscenities at people."

Silence filled the airwaves. It was coming. No way would Schmille sit back and take a lashing. Jackson knew him better than that. He would not only have something to say; he'd retaliate. He'd seen it happen to a lot of other guys on the force since Schmille had been promoted to captain.

"Archer, get to the station. You're on administrative leave. Effective immediately."

"On what grounds?" Jackson's jaw tightened. He wasn't backing down.

"Insubordination. I want your badge and service weapon on my desk."

"Be my pleasure, Captain."

Jackson hung up without waiting for another snarky comment. He'd never liked Rusty Schmille, and he thought even less of him now. He'd turn in his badge and his gun, but it wouldn't be until after he found Allison.

He grabbed his personal truck keys and started thinking about what Schmille had said. She'd been seen at a convenience store. He'd search all the stores in the area until her found her.

Jackson raced to the Quick-E Mart on Highway 183. It was the closest one to his house. Time was crucial, and he didn't feel like wasting it driving around from one convenience store to the next.

Jackson pulled in to the parking lot and saw police officers from his department working the scene. He pulled around the opposite side of the lot and parked at the back of the store where he could watch without being seen. There was no sign of Allison. Maybe she was still here. Jackson climbed out and walked to the edge of the trees behind the building. In the brief time they'd known each other, he'd come to learn a few things about her. One was that he knew she was scared out of her mind, and the second was that she hardly knew how to use a gun. Which made coming up on her in the woods a dangerous situation.

He'd have to take his chances. It wouldn't be long before other officers were searching for her, too. As he set out behind the store, he scanned the trees hoping to see her. Even though the morning sun was out, a winter wind whipped the air. He hoped she wasn't freezing somewhere. As he stepped over a big rock, something caught his eye.

Brown dots decorated one rock and a brown smudge on another. A flat rock a few feet ahead showed a faint outline of a small foot. She was hurt. Guilt lodged in his throat. If something happened to her, he would never forgive himself. He'd promised to keep her safe. Jackson stared at the rock and then gazed up into the grove of trees. Allison wasn't a country girl, so whatever path she took would probably be the one that was the easiest.

He heard officers behind him as they searched the woods. Jackson made his way through a clearing in the trees and raced ahead of them. As he fought his way deeper into the woods, he thought he heard a twig snapping to his right. Jackson spun around drawing his weapon.

The sight of her almost brought him to his knees. He holstered the gun and walked toward her. She was shivering with her knees tucked under her arms and her head buried into her chest. He took his coat off and bent down to wrap it around her. He pulled her to him and sat on the ground next to her.

"I-I-I knew it was you. I saw you behind m-me so I stopped and waited for you to catch up." Her teeth chattered with every word.

"Shh." He held her against his body as he rubbed her back trying to warm her up. Jackson brushed her hair from her face and kissed her forehead. "You're okay. I'm here now."

She nodded. "I didn't know if you'd find me. I kept moving but my feet are hurting so much." She glanced down. "I had to rest."

Jackson fought the emotions raging inside him. This could have easily turned out for the worst. All because of him. If only he'd made sure she was safe in his house. This was all his fault.

Now he had to think of a plan to get her out of there. He didn't want to turn her over to the feds because he knew what they would do to her. The questioning and the interrogation would be more than she could take. Especially right now.

"Allison, I need you to stay here for a few more minutes."

She began to shake her head. She looked up at him. Her eyes wide with fear. "No, p-please."

He lifted her chin with his index finger. Brown eyes pleaded with him. "Listen to me. There's a neighborhood right over there. I'm going to go drive my truck onto that street and come from over there to pick you up." He nodded toward the back of the grove of trees. "No one will see us. I'll take you somewhere safe."

"No, they'll find me again." She wiggled to pull away from him.

Jackson pulled her to him and held her tight. "All right." He buried his face into her neck. "I'm so sorry I let that happen to you." Her body relaxed into his.

She didn't say another word, and he didn't want her to. His lame apology couldn't convey the amount of guilt he was feeling. Nothing he could say would make up for what had happened to her.

"We'll go to my parents' house. It's only about twenty miles from here. No one will know to look for us there."

"I trust you, Jackson."

"Will you be all right while I go get my truck?"

"Sure. But please hurry."

Hearing her say she trusted him felt like a sucker punch to the gut. He'd let her down too many times. He wanted to promise that she'd be safe, but so far, he hadn't been able to keep any of the promises he'd made.

"I'll be coming back for you from that direction over there. You'll need to watch for me."

She pulled away from his arms and covered her face with her hands. Pain creased her features, although it didn't look like a physical pain.

"Jackson, I couldn't do it. They could've killed me,

but I just couldn't do it. I couldn't shoot so I ran as fast as I could."

He grabbed her wrists and kissed the back of each hand as she sobbed into her palms. "Let's talk about it later, Allison. You didn't do anything wrong. Just trust me. I'll explain everything later."

She uncovered her face and wiped her eyes. "How do you do it? I couldn't do your job."

"I don't know." At the moment, he didn't feel as if he deserved her admiration. Not after he'd allowed her to be here in the first place. "I'll be right back." Jackson stood up and took a last look at her. She was curled up in his black coat, shivering on the ground. He hoped he never had to see her that vulnerable again. He'd do whatever it took to keep her safe.

He raced to his truck and drove to the neighborhood behind the wooded area where she waited. It took him less than five minutes to get back to where she lay shivering on the rocks.

"See, I told you I'd be back soon." Jackson bent down and scooped her up in his arms. Allison wrapped hers around his neck.

"You don't have to carry me."

"I saw your feet. That's how I knew you were out there. You left bloody footprints on the rocks. I also knew if I didn't get ahead of them, they'd get to you first. I'm sure they saw them, too."

She lifted a leg and looked at her left foot. "I forgot about them. They're so cold I can't feel them anymore."

"I can't stand seeing you like this. As soon as I get you to my parents' house, you'll be able to rest.

"Are you sure they won't be upset that you're bringing a total stranger into their house?"

Jackson thought about how his parents would react. His dad would rail him for it. He already knew that. Especially after he told them about Schmille putting him on administrative leave. His mom would be asking a million questions, but she'd be more concerned about the fact that he had a woman with him. Either way, he was going to get blasted with questions from both of them.

"No, they won't mind a bit."

"Really?" She smiled and laid her forehead against his cheek. "They're going to be upset. I can see it in your face."

Jackson laughed. "Well, it won't be the first time."

They emerged from the trees and he carried her to his truck parked on the side of the road. He fumbled with the door handle so he wouldn't have to make her stand on her bruised and cut feet. The door swung open, and he set her down on the seat. He rushed around and turned on the ignition so he could get the heat blowing on her.

"Jackson."

He stared at her waiting to hear what she had to say.

"You saved my life."

A lump closed off his words. He gazed at her messy hair, brown eyes smudged with mascara and bloody feet.

He couldn't say a word.

But he knew this would be the last time anyone ever hurt Allison.

TWELVE

His cologne filled her senses and she inhaled it deep into her lungs. It was a scent she'd never forget. It was distinctly Jackson Archer.

"Still cold? I can turn the heat up if you want."

"No, I'm fine. My teeth finally stopped chattering."

He only nodded.

She could tell he felt horrible for what had happened to her, but there was no blame to be placed on him. What she couldn't understand was how they'd found her. Whoever these people were, they weren't giving up until she was dead. Allison turned to stare out the window. How long could she run? Sooner or later they'd have to give up. Or get caught.

"Do you think they'll ever stop looking for me?" She continued to stare out the window, afraid of what his answer was going to be.

"Depends."

She let out a breath. His short replies were hard to take. In the few days she'd known him she'd learned the shorter they were, the more brutal they were to hear.

"On what?"

"A lot of things."

"Like?"

He shot her an unreadable glance, but this time she didn't think it was anger or irritation.

"Us finding them before they find you."

"Oh."

She felt defeated. She was all cried out and exhausted from lack of sleep. His blunt answers weren't helping either, but she always respected his honesty.

"You'll be safe at my parents' house."

"I trust you, Jackson. It's just that…how long can I keep running?"

The realization that he was in his own personal vehicle and wearing plain clothes finally hit her. "Are you off duty now?"

"You could say that."

He was being evasive, again but this time she wasn't giving up until he told her the whole truth.

"Yeah, I could say that, but should I?"

Jackson chuckled under his breath and turned to grin at her.

"You've been around me too long already."

For once, the smile on his lips reached his eyes. The spark of playfulness took her by surprise. A gentleness in his green eyes hit her right in the heart.

"I was put on administrative leave."

The spark in his eyes faded. His face hardened, and there was the Jackson she'd come to know.

"What? Why?"

"Long story."

"It's because of me, isn't it?"

He shot her a look of irritation. "No."

"Then why? What did you do wrong? You were saving my life. How can that be wrong?"

"Protocol. I'm sure you've heard of that."

"Yes." The thought of Jackson losing his job because of her was the final straw. "I can't let you lose your job because of me."

"I'm not going to. Besides, if I did, it wouldn't be your fault.

Not her fault? It was her life they were trying to save. It was absolutely because of her. "I beg to differ."

"I don't want to talk about this, okay?"

"Jackson, I can't let you lose your job."

"Allison, it's not open for discussion. The conversation is over. You haven't done anything wrong."

"Why are you so stubborn?"

His cheeks reddened with anger. She noticed his grip tighten on the steering wheel. Regret seeped into every part of her. Nausea rolled in her stomach as she awaited the onslaught of words about to come out of his mouth. She wished she could snap her fingers and erase the words she'd spoken. She opened her mouth to apologize.

"Don't."

Jackson didn't finish the sentence, and he didn't need to. What he left unsaid spoke louder to her than words could have. She dared not reply and hoped her silence conveyed that she was apologetic. He was a man of few words, but one who could get a message across quicker than anyone she knew.

She respected that about him, but at the same time it was hard to discuss serious matters with him. They rode the next few miles in silence. His occasional humming was the only sound he made. As torturous as it was, she wasn't going to say another word until he said it first.

He pulled off the road and eased into a dollar-store

parking lot. "Stay here. Keep your head down. Just in case."

Allison crouched down in the seat while she waited for him to come back. A car door slammed next to her, causing her to jump. Being alone in the truck made her realize how much she needed him. If she ever wanted to get out of this alive, he was her only hope.

Ten agonizing minutes later, he came out with two white plastic bags full of items. "Here." He handed them to her.

She opened one of the bags to find a pair of socks, a roll of paper towels, hydrogen peroxide and antibiotic ointment. He'd obviously been more bothered by her injured feet than she'd realized.

"Thank you." She opened the other bag to find a pair of gray sweatpants, a matching zip-up hoodie and a pink T-shirt. He'd even thrown in a pair of slippers, hairbrush, mascara and lip gloss. In the very bottom of the bag was a bottle of scented body spray.

"Wow. I must really look a mess. And obviously I smell just as bad."

He shook his head and grinned. "Only a woman can take a kind gesture and turn it into an insult. Just hurry and clean your feet. Sorry about the slippers. I don't know what size shoe you wear. I figured those would fit better."

His tone turned icy. "We're almost to my parents' house. Don't ask questions about my wife or my daughter. Please?"

Allison's heart shattered at the tone in his voice. She wouldn't dare do that to him, but she knew why he felt the need to say it. "I wouldn't do that, anyway."

"I know. I just feel like I have to ask. I'm going to

need to pull over for a second and make a phone call. I don't have a strong cell reception right now, and it only gets worse from here."

Jackson eased the truck off the road and put it into Park. His green eyes settled on her face and lingered there.

"I don't know how you've put up with me. I've never met anyone like you before, Allison."

His tone was soft as it poured over her. "Is that good or bad?" She gave a nervous laugh.

"I don't know yet." He smiled, then turned to open the door. "I need to stand out of the truck to get better reception, but I'll be right here. I'm not letting you out of my sight. Ever again."

"Same here." The thought of being with Jackson Archer forever actually wasn't such a bad idea.

Jackson walked to the back of the truck and leaned against the tailgate. He watched Allison through the back window. It amazed him that a traffic call had turned into this.

It was time to clear his mind off Allison and refocus. He was anxious to find out what was going on with the case. Devon hadn't called yet, and he was starting to worry. Something didn't feel right. It wasn't like Devon to do this. Jackson dialed the number and waited.

"Hello?" A female voice answered.

"Hey, it's Jackson. Karen? Why are you answering Devon's phone?"

"Jackson. I'm so glad it's you."

Silence hung between them for a few seconds. His gut told him what his mind refused to believe. Something bad had happened. That's why Devon hadn't called.

"Is Devon okay?" He braced for the bad news.

"He's been shot, Jackson. He's out of surgery but it's still critical. He woke up once and asked for you. Said he had something to tell you about the case. He's been in and out, fighting the pain."

Jackson doubled over to catch his breath. *Lord, please don't let him die.* He stood up and steadied himself against the truck.

"I had no idea. How did it happen?" He had a million questions, but he knew Karen wouldn't have the answers.

"I don't have any answers for you. The only thing I can tell you is that Devon was at a red light coming into town. The weird thing was that he was driving Richard Maber's truck. I was hoping you would know what was going on."

"I'll be there as soon as I can. But I can't come to the hospital right now. It's too risky."

"What do you mean? Is Devon safe here?"

Her voice was on the verge of hysteria. He wished he could tell her yes, but he would be lying.

"Call and insist the department put someone outside his hospital door."

"Why can't you do it for him? Please, Jackson. You're scaring me."

"I can't. Schmille put me on administrative leave."

"What? Well, I'm not telling Devon right now. It'll only rile him up."

"No, don't. There's nothing he can do, anyway."

"Do you know who shot my husband?"

"No, but we'll find them."

"Listen, I don't repeat anything I hear you guys talking about. Ever. But Devon isn't thinking straight on the pain meds and anesthesia. He said something about a crooked cop and how it was time for a shakedown, and then he said a name."

Jackson's stomach lurched. It felt as if someone had kicked him in the gut.

"Did you recognize it?"

"Yes, Schmille. He couldn't say anything else. He was too out of it."

The blood drained from Jackson's head, leaving him dizzy. He always knew there was something about that man he didn't like or trust. That had to be how they kept finding Allison.

"Karen, did he say anything else?"

"No, he didn't mention any other names. Oh, wait. He said something about Al. He was mumbling but it sounded like he said, 'Jackson, be careful, Al,' but he was in and out at that time so I'm not sure if that's exactly what he said."

"Thanks, Karen. I'll be there as soon as I can."

Jackson's heart sank. Be careful of Allison? But why? Was she involved in this somehow? Was she masterminding this whole thing? That couldn't have been what Devon meant.

Jackson watched through the back glass as Allison brushed her hair. She must've caught him in the visor mirror because she turned to look back at him. Could he have been wrong about her?

Allison opened the passenger door and walked around the back of the truck. Her slippers scuffed against the gravel. She placed a hand on his arm. "Are you okay?"

He looked into her eyes. The cold wind whipped the hair around her face. Devon's comments left him wondering about a lot. Whatever he'd meant, Jackson didn't want to believe Allison was guilty of anything other than being at the wrong place at the wrong time.

But he didn't trust his own judgment anymore, especially where it came to Allison. He'd made some rash decisions the past few days. They'd all been because of her. She was getting to him in ways he had never imagined or expected.

"Yeah. Everything's fine."

She smiled. "I watched you while you were talking. Your face looked pretty serious."

"Nothing to worry about. Let's get back in the truck. We're burning daylight."

He watched her scuffle back to the truck in the slippers he'd bought her. A few days ago he was planning a fishing trip with his brother. It was crazy how fast life could change. He couldn't wait to get her off the road and settled in at his parents' house. No one would find them there. Or at least he hoped not.

A few minutes after they'd gotten back on the road, Jackson turned onto a long dirt driveway lined with mesquite trees. At the end stood a white two-story farmhouse with a large front porch. She noticed rocking chairs on each side. It was like a picture right out of a southern magazine.

"This is beautiful. Did you grow up here?"

"No, they bought this place after Dad retired. They aren't farmers. They lease the land to the neighbor's son. He farms cotton on it every other year. They just enjoy the quiet country life. It didn't surprise me when they settled out here."

"I love it."

"It's pretty secluded. Which is why you're here, so don't try to access the internet, cell phones or anything else."

"Do you think they could track me down out here?"

"Mom and Dad have a high-tech security system and a Great Dane named Sugar who likes to bite strangers. Just relax and get some rest until I figure out our next move. When I know what that is, I'll tell you. You deserve to have some rest. Take advantage of it."

Allison blew out a ragged breath. "I can't relax. Now I have to worry about Sugar eating me like a snack when I get out of the truck."

Jackson laughed. "She's well trained to take commands, so you'll be fine."

She loved animals, so she hoped he was right. Meeting his family had her stomach in knots. As if she wasn't a wreck already, the thought of being around his parents was almost as scary as running from a killer.

He pulled up to the house. "Just giving you a heads-up. I haven't seen them in a while. I don't want to scare them with the truth. I'm going to go in first. You stay out here and change your clothes. Whatever you do, don't tell them what happened to you."

"I won't. But don't you think they will ask?"

"Sure, they will. They're my parents. I've decided we're going to let them think whatever they want. If they ask, I'll tell them the truth. I don't want to stress them out by telling them what's really happening, unless they ask me. I can't lie to my parents."

How in the world was he going to pull this off?

There was no way his parents would believe they just came for a visit. She hadn't known him for long, but she knew his parents would be shocked to see him with a woman. He'd never be able to fool them with this.

"I know what you're thinking."

She laughed. "No, I don't think you do."

"You're thinking I can't pull this off."

She nodded. "Well, yeah. That's exactly what I was thinking."

He opened the truck door and glanced back at her. He winked and shot her a playful grin. "I've got this. Wait here. I'll be right back."

Allison's heart skipped a few beats as she watched him shut the door and walk up to the house. He was a man of many layers. But one thing she'd discovered was that he was a man of integrity. And like it or not, she completely trusted him with her life.

The front door of the house opened, and a dark-haired woman, who looked exactly like Jackson, wrapped her arms around his neck and kissed his cheek. She led him into the house and shut the door.

Allison sank down in the front seat and wriggled out of the ragged clothes she was still wearing. She slipped on the shirt and sweat suit, cleaned her feet, and spritzed on a little body spray. She sat back up on the seat and pulled the visor down so she could use the mirror.

The sight of her reflection was frightening. Dark circles hung under her eyes, making her face look paler than normal. No amount of makeup could cover what she'd been through. She dabbed on some mascara and lip gloss hoping it would help a little. Last, she pulled the slippers back on and waited for him to come out to get her.

The front door finally opened. A gigantic black dog lunged onto the porch and then raced for the truck. The dog braced its lanky body against the window and stared right at her. She'd managed to escape a killer more times than she was willing to count, and now she was about to get eaten by an oversized house pet.

"Sugar! Get down!"

A gray-haired man stood on the porch yelling. This had to be Jackson's father, but there was hardly a resemblance. There was no doubt that he got his looks from his mother.

The dog slid down the window and ran back to the porch. Jackson walked out behind his dad and motioned to her. He was out of his mind if he thought she was getting out of the truck. Jackson motioned to her again. She shook her head. She wasn't getting out if that dog was around. He jogged down the steps toward the truck and opened the passenger side door.

"Come on, Allison. It's time to meet my parents."

"What about that horse they keep in the house?"

Jackson laughed. His face looked more relaxed than she'd ever seen it. She could already tell that being with his family was good for him.

"Sugar won't hurt you. As long as you're with the family, she knows you're okay." He reached out to take her hand. "Let's go."

Family? Allison looked down at his hand over hers. For a second, all the pain and terror she'd been feeling vanished. She wished they could stay like this forever.

"Okay, let's do this."

THIRTEEN

Jackson knew touching her hand was taking a huge risk. He knew bringing her here under the premise of a relationship was like walking blindfolded into a fire. Somehow, he'd have to tell his parents the truth, but he didn't like the idea of worrying his mom. If they asked, and they would, he would tell them everything. He knew they would respect the fact that he wasn't going to let anything else happen to Allison. He'd make sure to put an end to this nightmare. Even if it meant losing his job. Which was unlikely, given the fact that Schmille would be on his way out once this whole thing was blown wide open.

"Are you totally sure that dog won't eat me alive?"

"Absolutely." He grinned. She was squeezing his hand like a lemon. "Unless you make me scream out in pain from that death grip you have on my hand. Sugar probably wouldn't like that very much."

She looked down and let his hand drop like a hot coal. "Sorry." Her face flushed.

"Come on, you've got to stay with me on this. You can't wimp out on me in front of my parents. I don't want to scare my mom into thinking something is wrong."

"I won't. I can do this." Her eyes met his with determination.

Jackson led her up the front steps where his parents stood ready to pounce. "Here it comes," he whispered through clenched teeth.

"Hi," his mother said, her arms outstretched to give Allison a hug.

He watched as Allison smiled back and allowed his mom to embrace her. She pulled away from Allison and placed a hand on his cheek. "Jackson, I'm so glad you brought her. Y'all come inside. We were just about to sit down to lunch. Let me make you both a sandwich and some soup. It's not much, but it'll warm you up."

"How's work, son?" his dad asked.

Jackson stepped aside to allow Allison to follow his mother into the house. He turned his face away from his dad before answering.

"Going great, Dad."

He knew one of his biggest flaws was not being able to put on a poker face in front of his parents. Somehow, they could always see a lie in his eyes.

The smell of tomato-basil soup and chicken panini filled the house. His mom was an excellent cook who'd always had a knack for making the smallest meal seem special.

"It smells so good in here." Allison trailed behind his mother toward the kitchen.

A strong hand grabbed Jackson's shoulder.

"Come here, son."

Jackson's stomach knotted. "Yeah, Dad?"

His father sat down in his favorite old brown recliner

and looked up at him. "Sit down. Let's do some catching up," he said, motioning toward the couch.

Jackson sat and waited for the questioning to begin. Being raised by an officer of the United States Army meant walking the straight-and-narrow line. Colonel Steven Archer didn't tolerate being lied to, especially not by his own children.

"What's on your mind, Dad?"

"What are you doing here, Jackson?"

And there it was. "We just came for a visit."

"Cut it out, son."

"Sir?"

"You heard me. What's she doing here? You and I both know that's not your girlfriend. Nothing against her, she seems nice and all, but you haven't brought a girl to meet us since Hope died. And I'm pretty sure you wouldn't bring one here wearing sweatpants and slippers."

His dad leaned forward and stared him in the eyes. Jackson's cheeks warmed and thought he felt beads of sweat forming at his hairline.

"So? What's going on, son?"

Jackson dragged both palms down his face, then rubbed the stubble on his cheeks. He blew out a ragged breath. "Yeah, okay. You're right. But Dad, you can't tell Mom yet. She'd be terrified if she knew the truth. I was going to tell you, but I don't want to worry her."

"Do you think I told your mother everything I did in the army? She won't ask if I tell her not to. Now what is going on?"

"It's a long story."

"Jackson!" His mother's voiced echoed from the kitchen. Two seconds later she appeared in the living room with her hands on her hips. "Jackson, it's rude to leave your guest. Come on, lunch is ready."

"We'll be right there, Lynda."

Jackson watched his parents exchange a look only the two of them could decipher. His mom walked away without saying another word.

His dad turned his gaze back on him. "You were saying?"

Jackson decided he'd better start at the beginning. He should've known this was going to happen. "Dispatch got a call two nights ago saying there was a woman reporting an overturned vehicle. When I went to check it out, I found Allison in her car. She'd crashed through Bob Langley's fence. She confirmed there was an overturned truck. She said a man inside was shooting at her. We checked it out and found a body inside. No sign of the man she talked about, but it turns out the body was an undercover DEA agent."

His dad interrupted. "And you trust this girl, Jackson? What were you thinking bringing her here?"

"Because they're trying to kill her."

His dad leaned back in his chair and stared at the ceiling for what felt like an eternity. He leveled his eyes on Jackson's face.

"Who's they?"

"I don't know. She's clean, Dad. She works for Paradigm Enterprises in Houston. Apparently, she does all kinds of administrative duties for them."

"Get to the point, Jackson."

His dad wasn't a man who liked waiting. Jackson cleared his throat and continued explaining. "She accidentally took a picture of the guy in the truck when she went to render aid. He started shooting at her, but she got away. I found out a little later that the man who tried to kill her is in the cartel. Someone also tried to kill her in the hospital."

"I trust you're doing whatever you can to keep her safe?"

"Of course."

"Then why is she here? Why didn't you hand her over to the feds? What makes you think you're better at this than they are?"

"We have a dirty cop in the department."

"And you know this for a fact?"

"Yes. Devon was shot, and he told his wife while he was under sedation."

"Devon? Is he going to be all right?"

"I hope so. He's critical. His wife said he was mumbling something about crooked cops. She said he mentioned Captain Schmille."

"How can you be sure they won't find her here? "

Jackson braced his elbows on his knees and rested his head in his hands. This was all starting to make sense. Now that he was able to say it all out loud, it was falling into place. He caught a glimpse of a family picture sitting on a bookshelf across the living room. His late wife and baby smiled back at him. Coming here was a big mistake.

"You're right, Dad. I shouldn't have come here with her. We need to leave." He started to stand.

"No, son. Sit down."

Images of his wife and daughter alive in his parents' house flashed through his mind. It was getting harder to breathe as the grief filled his lungs. Whoever said time eased the pain had never lost a family.

"Jackson."

He felt his dad's hand on his arm. He eased back down on the couch.

His father's hand rested firmly on his knee, squeezing it to get his attention. "Son, look at me."

Jackson lifted his eyes to his father's face.

"I don't know what's going on, but I can tell it's got you a wreck. Stay here for the night. Get some sleep. You'll be safe here."

He desperately needed some sleep and some time to think, but he couldn't stay. "We could all be in danger. Even you and Mom. They keep finding us. This time I didn't tell anyone where we were going, so we should be okay. I'm on leave so I didn't check in."

His dad tapped Jackson's arm and shook his head to signal him to stop talking.

"Steven and Jackson! Lunch is ready!" His mom appeared in the living room. She watched the two of them for a second, then disappeared back into the kitchen.

"Come on, son. Eat, rest. We'll talk more later, but not in front of your mother."

Sleep would give his mind some clarity. He needed to figure out a lot of things, and he needed to check on Devon again while they were here. As he stepped into the kitchen, he saw his mom and Allison giggling like a couple of schoolgirls. Something his mom had never done with Hope. Allison looked up to catch him staring.

"Hey, your mom was just telling me stories about you."

"Great, Mom. Why don't you break out the photo albums?"

His mom giggled and winked at Allison. "Too late."

"You were so cute when you were little." Allison held up a baby picture of Jackson.

"Say it ain't so, Mom." He walked to the table and sat down next to her. He reached out and snatched the picture from Allison's hand. "Let me see that."

Jackson studied the picture. It was of a dark-haired little boy about three years old. He was wearing super-hero underwear and sitting on a tricycle. He couldn't help but laugh.

"Mom, that's not me." He tossed the picture onto the table. "That's Eric."

His mom grabbed the photo and stared closely at it for a few seconds. "No kidding? Wow, you boys look more alike than I ever realized."

"Allison, where are you from?" his dad asked.

"I grew up in Houston."

"Any family there?" His mother fired off a question as she plated the food.

Jackson watched pain settle over Allison's features. He knew she missed her family and her home.

"No, my parents live in New Mexico."

"That's nice. Any brothers or sisters?"

"Yes, I have one sister. She lives in Stonewater. She has two little girls. In fact, she had a baby recently. I was supposed to be there for the birth. But I caught the flu and missed it."

"Oh, I'm sorry to hear that, dear. How about some sweet tea?"

"Yes, thank you."

Jackson noticed the sadness on Allison's face. Most women wouldn't have held up as well as Allison in this situation. He admired her strength.

They all sat down as his mom poured four glasses of tea and set them on the table in front of them. After lunch was over and they had cleared the dishes, his mom showed Allison to a spare bedroom so she could rest. Jackson sat on the porch sipping a cup of coffee with one hand and scratching Sugar's head with the other.

The front door creaked open and his dad joined him.

"Mind if I sit with you?"

"Not at all." Jackson scooted over on the porch swing. His dad eased down next to him. Sugar laid her head in his lap waiting for a good ear rub.

"She's spoiled rotten," Jackson said. Sugar shot a look at him as if she understood him.

"Allison's a tough girl. She held it in, but you can tell she's been through a lot lately."

Jackson wasn't the only one who'd noticed Allison's brave front. "Yeah, she has. She thinks the cartel is after her for accidentally taking a picture of the man in the truck. I didn't tell her any differently, but if that's all it was, they wouldn't be able to find her so easily. I wish I knew why this was happening."

"Your mother and I will be praying for her. While we're talking about her, what's really between the two of you?"

"Not a thing. I was moving her to a safe house when they came after us. One thing after another led us here."

"Well, I like her."

Jackson couldn't help but notice how his parents took to her.

"Mom sure liked her. She was never like that with Hope."

His dad cleared his throat. "You know why that is, Jackson?"

"No, I really don't know, Dad. Why?"

"She loved Hope, but Hope was always jealous of

you being so close to your family. She didn't have much of a family, so we bent over backward to include her. I don't think she meant it, but I think she was always a little jealous."

Jackson stood from the swing. Sugar moved out of his way to go lay on the welcome mat. "I don't like you talking about Hope like that, Dad."

"Come on, Jackson. You need to talk about her. You've run away from this for too long now. Allison is a sweet girl. There's nothing wrong with you having a woman in your life."

His dad sounded like everyone else. Why was it so important to talk about something that hurt so much?

"Dad, I'm okay. I don't really need to talk about it. I've accepted it as much as any man can."

His dad stood up and walked to the door, shoving Sugar out of the way with the toe of his boot. "Mark the blameless and behold the upright, for there is a future for the man of peace. Psalm 37:37." His dad patted him on the shoulder. "Find your peace, son. It's time."

He watched his dad take Sugar inside. He was glad to be left alone. Jackson sat back down on the swing and thought about those words. Maybe his dad was right. It had been years, and he was still wallowing in his self-pity. His heart yearned to talk to God about it, but he still felt too vulnerable. He wasn't ready to bare his heart to God or anyone else. He closed his eyes to shut the world out. A few minutes later, the creaking front door jarred him back to reality.

"Jackson, can I join you?"

His eyes flew open. Allison's sweet voice ran down his back.

"Sure." He moved over to give her space.

"Your parents are really great. They're so kind." Her voice cracked. She turned away and cleared her throat.

"Thank you. I should visit them more often. I feel bad that I don't."

"I know what you mean. Same here. I miss my parents. The past few days have made me see how much I have taken my family for granted. I hope I get to see them again."

Her resolve crumbled and she buried her face in her hands. Jackson put his arm around her shoulder and pulled her into him.

"I'm sorry this has happened to you," he whispered. He kissed the top of her head.

She pulled away, wiped her cheeks, then turned to him. Jackson brushed a stray tear from her face with his finger. For the first time in a long time, his heart longed for a woman in his life.

"How do you do it?"

Her question brought him back to his senses. "Do what?"

"Deal with criminals and dangerous people."

She looked at him, waiting for an answer. Only he didn't have one. He didn't want to answer her question. He only wanted to think about what he was feeling sitting in the swing next to her. He pulled her into him and lifted her chin with his finger.

She stared up at him. Confused. Afraid. He didn't really know what he was seeing in her eyes, but he didn't care to figure it out.

He brushed a kiss across her lips. The familiar softness of a woman's mouth made him wonder if he was dreaming. He'd never had these feelings for any woman since meeting Hope. As familiar as kissing a woman's lips felt, it was also new and exciting. And if he had to be honest, it was scary.

But it felt right.

Allison placed a hand on his cheek and returned the kiss. After what felt like minutes, she pulled back. Her finger traced the line of his jaw as her eyes followed.

"You are the most handsome…most confusing…" She stopped and grinned. "And I must add *moodiest* man I've ever met."

Jackson laughed. "Then I'm surprised you didn't slap me for kissing you."

"Why did you?"

This woman. Why couldn't she let him feel what he wanted without analyzing his every word or action? Thinking about why he kissed her wasn't something he felt like doing.

Before he could answer, she sprang from the swing. "You know what, let's forget that it happened. It's okay. Really. I know we're both under a lot of stress right now."

He pulled both hands down his face and moaned. "Stop, Allison. Please."

Jackson grabbed her hand and pulled her back down to the swing. "Allison, I kissed you because I wanted to. If you make me think about it more than that, it'll just make me second-guess everything I say or do from here on out. I wanted to and I liked it."

He leaned forward and kissed her cheek and then brushed another kiss over her mouth. "And that one is because *you* wanted me to." Jackson stood and headed toward the front door. He stopped and smiled when he noticed the flush on her cheeks. "I'm starving." He winked at her, then went inside.

* * *

A newfound anxiousness swept over her. Unsure if she needed to laugh or cry, she pulled her knees up to her chest and wrapped her arms around her legs. She stared across the landscape, reliving the kiss over and over in her mind.

Somehow, in the middle of running for their lives, she'd fallen for this man. A cop with an attitude as big as Texas. She wondered how this thing between them would end. How this would all end. Deep in her soul she knew she would be all right. Her faith in God was the only thing keeping her going. Even if those lunatics did kill her, her faith told her she'd have eternal life. But if she made it through this ordeal, would she have Jackson?

There were so many unanswered questions, but for now she needed to relax. She stood from the swing and headed toward the door. Something rustled in the distance. Allison stopped, frozen with fear. The pale light of dusk made it hard to see more than shadows. It was probably her imagination. Besides, Jackson promised her no one would find them out here.

"Who's there?" Her voice shook with fear. The silence felt as if it had swallowed her up whole. The snapping of a twig sent her racing across the porch. Allison threw the front door open and ran face first into Jackson's chest. His strong arms wrapped around her and held her to him.

"Whoa. What's got you scared?" His tone was thick with concern.

Her heart hammered in her ears. "I heard something." She fought to catch her next breath.

Worry etched across his face. "Like what?"

"Rustling. Snapping. I called out to see if someone was out there, but no one answered me. I thought you said no one would find us here." She fought to catch her breath.

"Stay inside the house. I'll take a look."

Allison watched him reach behind his back to pull out a pistol. He obviously knew as well as she did that they weren't safe anywhere.

"Allison, come in and have a cup of coffee with us before dinner." His mother motioned for her to come into the kitchen.

Her stomach knotted at the invitation. She didn't want to tell his mom that her son was in the front yard looking for a killer. Sitting down to coffee wasn't something she could do while Jackson was out there putting himself in danger.

"Oh, no thank you. I can't have caffeine this late in the afternoon. I'll never sleep tonight."

"Don't be silly. It's decaf. I have a chocolate cake to go with it. Come on in here."

Every second with Jackson out there seemed like one too many. Allison tried to smile as if nothing was wrong. "Thank you. I'd love some cake. Chocolate is my favorite."

She followed his mother into the kitchen and sat at the table. A mug of coffee and a piece of cake were already waiting for her.

"I don't know what you like in your coffee, dear. I left it black. We have sugar and artificial sweetener, cream, flavored syrups. How would you like it?"

Allison hardly heard a word as she focused on the sound of Jackson coming through the front door.

"Allison?"

"Oh, uh, black is fine. Thank you."

Steven Archer's laughter filled the kitchen. "I read an article the other day about how psychopaths drink black coffee."

"Steven! That's rude."

Under normal circumstances Allison would've found that funny. Right now, the only thing she wanted to hear was the sound of Jackson coming back inside.

The back door to the kitchen opened and Jackson walked in. "What's so funny?"

Allison fought the urge to run to him and wrap her arms around his neck. She let out a breath and sank down into her chair.

His mom piped up. "Oh, you know your dad. His idea of funny isn't always funny."

"He thinks I'm a psychopath because I drink my coffee black."

"You know, I read an article about that the other day."

Laughter boomed around the kitchen.

"Like father, like son." His mother shook her head.

Allison couldn't help but laugh. She liked his parents. It wasn't hard to tell that he'd been raised in a wonderful, loving home. Jackson walked around the table to take a seat next to her. As he passed her, he leaned down and whispered in her ear.

"It's all good." He grinned just before grabbing her plate of cake. "Thanks." He shoved a big bite into his mouth.

"Jackson, that was for Allison," his mother scolded him like he was a five-year-old.

Sugar's bark reverberated around the kitchen and ev-

eryone froze. The massive dog barreled from the room
with her teeth bared.

Jackson bolted from his chair. "Stay here!"

"I'm going with you. It's my house," Steven said.

Jackson grabbed Allison's arm. "Whatever you hear,
please don't go out there."

FOURTEEN

"Dad, stay with Mom."

Jackson went into the living room and peered out of the front door window. Sugar stood next to him still baring her teeth.

His dad emerged from the hallway carrying a hunting rifle. "Dad, no. Stay here with Mom. I've got this."

"Don't talk back to me, son."

A scream came from the kitchen. Jackson raced past his dad. Allison met him as she bolted from the kitchen.

"What happened?"

His dad stood behind him with a rifle pointed at the door. "What'd you hear, Lynda?"

"Someone tried to come in through the back door."

"Are you sure?" Jackson looked at Allison. Fear shone in her eyes.

Lynda nodded. "The doorknob rattled. I always keep it locked. I'm setting the alarm. No one will get in here without us knowing it." His mom walked to the panel on the kitchen wall and engaged the alarm system. "The code is Archer spelled backward, in case you need it, Jackson."

A quietness settled over the room. Jackson looked around the kitchen. "Where's Sugar?"

"Did you let her out?" His dad ran back to the living room.

Panic knotted Jackson's stomach, and he raced toward the front door right on his dad's heels. The dog wasn't in the house.

"Dad, I didn't let her out. I know for a fact the door was closed. She was standing right behind me when I looked out the window."

"Turn the alarm off, Lynda!"

"Steven, no!"

"Now, Lynda. Sugar is outside."

His mom didn't ask questions. She disarmed the system and stood in the living room, her face pale. Allison hovered behind her.

"Can she open the door?" Jackson felt the door knob for teeth marks.

"She never has before." His dad shot him a concerned look.

"Stay here. I'll go find her."

Jackson opened the front door, his pistol extended as his eyes swept the porch. He stepped over the threshold. "Sugar!" He called out the dog's name a few more times. Nothing. "Dad, flip on the floodlight."

The front yard brightened with a soft yellow hue. Jackson eased down the steps. A bump sounded from the side of the house. He swallowed hard. How could they have found them here? If he'd put his parents' lives in danger, he'd never forgive himself.

Heavy breathing sounded behind him. Jackson spun around. Out of the darkness something knocked him off balance. It took him a second to realize it was the dog.

"Sugar." Trying to catch his breath, he steadied himself against the dog's lunges. "Come on, girl. Let's get you back inside."

Jackson led the dog into the house and shut the door. This time he locked it. "Turn the alarm back on, Mom."

"How in the world did she get out?"

Jackson examined the doorknob. There weren't any teeth marks or scratches, no sign of a dog's mouth prying its way out.

His dad walked up behind him. "She didn't get out on her own. Someone had to open the front door and let her out."

"Mom, Allison, stay in the kitchen with Sugar." Jackson turned to his dad. "We need to search this house."

Jackson searched the guest bedrooms while his father searched the rest of the house. After looking in closets, under beds and behind every curtain, they were both satisfied no one was inside.

His dad met him back in the hallway. "Any signs of someone in here?"

"No. I'll stay up tonight in case they come back."

His dad nodded. "How do you think they're finding you?"

"I don't know, Dad. I made a mistake coming here. We need to leave."

"They can't get in here without us knowing it. This alarm system is state-of-the-art. And we'll shoot them if they do."

"I don't know how they're finding us. No one knew we were coming here. Not even Devon."

"Turn your phone off."

Jackson pulled his phone from his pocket. How could

he have been so careless? He turned it off and shoved it into his pocket. "I hardly get a signal out here, so I didn't think someone could track my phone."

"Maybe not, but you need to be careful. Stay here tonight. I'll stay up with you. It's not safe for you to leave with her right now. The cover of darkness only gives them the advantage."

"After dinner I want you and Mom to leave. You'll have to tell her everything."

His dad didn't argue. "Let's go eat the dinner your mother cooked, and then I'll tell her what is going on. She won't be happy. Although, she's been admiring that new luxury hotel they built in Austin, so maybe I'll take her there to get her mind off of it. But before I go, I have something that will help you."

They all went into the kitchen and sat down to dinner. The conversation was strained, but his mom did the best she could to make everyone feel comfortable. Jackson cleared the table off for her and Allison helped her wash the dishes. When the last plate was put away, he said her name.

"Allison, I can show you to your room if you'd like to get some sleep."

The wide-eyed look on her face said she wasn't about to close her eyes after the scare they'd had. "Oh, sure."

"Good night, dear. Sleep well." Lynda hugged Allison, then began to fill Sugar's food and water bowls as she scolded the oversize animal for getting out.

Allison followed him down the long hallway to the guest room. Once inside, Jackson shut the door and turned to face her.

"That dog didn't get out on her own, did she?" Allison whispered.

"No."

She began to pace the room. "What are we going to do?"

Jackson reached out to snag her arm. "Hey, stop for a second. I have a plan. Sit down." He sat on the bed and patted a space next to him.

Allison sat down facing him. "What is it?"

He handed her a small device he'd gotten from his dad.

"What's this?"

"It's a GPS tracker. Dad had it on my mom's car. It's small enough for you to hide in your pocket. Keep it on you at all times."

"I don't understand. Do you think they'll find me here?"

"Yes." He hated to admit the truth to her, but he was pretty sure they already had.

"And this is all you're doing about it? Giving me something to carry so you'll be able to find my dead body?"

"Allison, it was Dad's idea. And I thought it was a good one. We know who we're dealing with. These people are relentless. They always know where to find you. I need to know where to find you, too."

He looked into her worried eyes. Seeing her talking with his parents over coffee and lunch had changed something inside of him. The wall around his heart was crumbling like a cookie. This woman had entered his life and turned it upside down. She put his life in danger, and now his parents' lives, too. And yet he felt more alive being with her than he had in five years.

She shifted on the bed. "Jackson, why are you staring at me?"

"What happened with your ex-fiancé?"

Shock registered on her face.

"I wasn't expecting you to ask me about that."

"What happened?"

"I don't like talking about it, but I'm going to make an exception for you." She stood from the bed and paced in front of him.

"He cheated on me. When I found out, I confronted him. He said a lot of mean things that crushed me. He tried to make me feel as if I had caused it in some way. All the blame was shifted to me. I think he wanted to be the one to break up first so it didn't hurt his ego. He was very controlling like that"

Heat crept up Jackson's neck. He'd never understand how some men viewed women as their property.

"He did you a favor, actually. You don't deserve to be treated that way. No woman does."

"I know that now. It was just a bad time in my life."

She stopped pacing. "Until this happened. This is by far the worst thing I've ever been through."

"I know. I have an idea about what's going on, but I don't have anyone sharing information with me now that Devon has been shot. I'm on administrative leave, so I'm not calling the station right now."

A gasp filled the room.

"Devon was shot?"

He realized he hadn't told her about Devon.

She sat on the bed next to him. Tears filled her eyes. "Why didn't you tell me? Is he going to be all right?" She hid her face with her hands. "It's all my fault."

Jackson wrapped his arms around her body, covering her as if shielding her from the world.

"No, it's not your fault. I'm sorry that I didn't tell

you. I didn't mean for you to find out this way. He's critical, but his wife said he's doing better."

"I'll be praying for him." She looked up and sniffed.

Jackson didn't reply, but he was glad she was praying for Devon. Since Hope and Natalie's death, he found it hard to pray. God didn't seem to hear his prayers, but maybe He would hear Allison's.

"What now?" She wiped her cheeks with the back of her hand.

"You get some sleep."

Jackson kissed her forehead. He got up and walked to the door. He took in the sight of her sitting on the bed. Her brown eyes, her mouth, her soft hair. She was beautiful inside and out, and he couldn't get enough of looking at her.

He wanted to promise her that no one would ever hurt her again. But after hearing what she'd been through, he couldn't do it. He'd already let her down more than once.

Fear weighed on him like a cold, wet blanket. He hadn't been able to save his own family, but that had been out of his control. This wasn't. He was going to save her.

He stopped in the doorway and turned back to face her. His heart longed to beg God for His protection, but the memories of his family stopped him.

Instead, he shut the door and walked away.

The soft bed cradled her aching body as she lay staring at the ceiling. She closed her eyes to pray, and after she said "Amen," she lay awake thinking about Jackson. He'd changed so much since she'd first met him on that cold, dark highway. It had been only a few days, yet somehow she felt like she'd known him for years. No one had ever made her feel as safe as Jackson Archer made her feel. She trusted him with her life, but trusting him with her heart was another matter.

As hard as she tried, she couldn't deny the attraction to him. But she also couldn't deny that he might always compare her to his late wife. Hope was perfect in every way. Beautiful, wealthy, successful. A good mother. They were complete opposites. On the surface it seemed like the past five years hadn't been enough time for him to grieve, and yet here he was kissing her. How could she trust his feelings?

It was too much to think about tonight. She needed to get some rest. If the past few days had taught her anything, it was that rest shouldn't be taken for granted. Wind chimes outside her window played a soft tune that lulled her to sleep.

Minutes after drifting off, Allison's eyes flew open. Something had jarred her from the dream she was having. She lay still, expecting a noise, hoping it was Sugar, or something more benign.

Allison's heart pounded in her chest as she sucked in deep breaths to calm its pace. She sat up in bed to calm herself down. Just as she felt relaxed enough to lie back down, the glow of the alarm clock went out, putting the room in complete darkness. She bolted upright. The power must've gone out.

Fear froze her to the bed. She hoped Jackson would rush in any minute to tell her to go back to sleep and relax. That it was nothing to worry about. What she wouldn't give to have his arms around her, protecting her. The bedroom door creaked open. Allison let out a long sigh of relief.

"What happened to the power?"

The dark figure entered the room but didn't respond.

"Jackson? What happened?"

Silence.

A hand wrapped around her face. She fought to pry the strong fingers from her mouth, but the attacker only tightened his grip.

"Don't fight it." A raspy male voice whispered in her ear.

She jerked to get away. Pain seared her head. What determination she had left disintegrated along with her consciousness.

Jackson's parents had left after Allison was settled into her room. They'd been gone only an hour, but he longed to call and check on them. Even though they weren't the ones the cartel was after, he still wanted to know they were safe. He could imagine the grief his mom was going through now that she knew the truth. He'd never meant to drag them into this. The next time he visited, he'd make sure it was on much better terms.

Jackson settled into his father's recliner. The clicking of the mantel clock attempted to lull him into a false sense of security. There was something about being in his parents' home that gave him a warm fuzzy feeling. But he wasn't a kid, and tonight had given him anything but the warm fuzzies.

Jackson fought to keep his eyes and ears open. He wanted nothing more than to prop up the foot of his dad's old chair and lay back for a long night's sleep. Instead, he shifted and sat up straighter as he strained his ears to hear past the tick-tock of the clock. He'd promised her that nothing would happen tonight. This time, he intended on keeping his word.

A loud beep broke through the quietness of the house, followed by an alert signaling that the security system was without power. He bolted from the chair and grabbed a flashlight from the coffee table drawer. Holding it with one hand and his gun in the other, he scanned the room to see if anyone was there.

Emotions took over and he raced toward the hallway. He noticed the bedroom door ajar.

"Allison, are you okay?"

When there wasn't an answer, he pushed the door with his boot. Something blocked it from opening farther. Jackson pushed it again, this time with more force.

Someone shoved it back. The flashlight fell to the floor and flickered out.

"Come out!"

A dark figure lunged from the bedroom. Jackson swung and missed, causing him to stagger. His first instinct was to shoot, but he didn't know where Allison was in the dark. He swung again. This time his fist contacted something solid and muscular. A large man. Pain seared his head, knocking him off his balance. Jackson grabbed for the wall.

"Allison, where are you?"

There was no reply. Something sharp pricked his hand. Jackson swung again but missed contact with anything solid. A fist landed on his jaw. He stumbled backward into the hallway. Somehow, the man hitting him seemed to have a greater advantage in the dark. Jackson strained to see into Allison's room. He thought he saw a large figure heading toward him. As it neared, he knew it wasn't her.

He lifted his gun and fired. The recoil sent his arms jerking into the air. Something hard and firm hit his head. The muscles in his arms felt leaden, and his legs buckled under his own weight. The blow rendered him dazed and weak.

Jackson braced himself against the door frame. He tried to call out her name, but something hit him again. This time from behind. Jackson sank to the floor. He fought waves of pain until the last thought he had was of finding whoever did this. Someone had to get to Allison. Jackson instinctively grabbed at his shoulder for his radio, then remembered he didn't have his equipment.

Defeat settled over him. He lay still, hoping the pain in his head would subside. "God, you don't have to save me unless I can save Allison. Please don't let her die."

If he was going to save her, he had to get off the floor. Mustering what little strength he had, he pulled himself up and waves of nausea forced him back down.

FIFTEEN

Musty air entered her lungs. Where was she? Darkness surrounded her.

Was she still at his parents' house? She couldn't hear Jackson's voice. Was he in the room?

Male voices sounded as if they were miles away. Her stomach twisted and lurched like a roller coaster. Her brain searched for answers. Why was everything so hazy? She blinked her eyes trying to focus, but the room was dark. She remembered about the power. It had gone out right before…she strained to remember what happened next.

"Jackson," she whispered. Her lips were dry, and her throat felt parched. She needed some water. Why wouldn't he answer?

Pain radiated through her leg. She couldn't tell if she'd been hit or kicked.

"Shut up!"

Fear squeezed her chest and robbed her of breath. It wasn't Jackson's voice she'd heard. The back of her head ached along with her leg.

"Where am I?" The smell of dirt filled her senses.

Pain shot through her leg again. Her eyes watered and she cried out.

"I said shut up!"

Everything in her wanted to scream, but she didn't dare make a sound.

She remembered now. The power had gone out. Fear filled her chest.

How could he have let this happen? "Jackson wouldn't let them take me," she whispered. Vertigo gripped her as she argued with herself.

It could mean only one thing. Something bad must have happened to him. If Jackson couldn't get to her, she would have to find a way to save herself.

Hair fell across her eyes, blocking her vision. She lifted her arm to wipe it away, then felt the back of her head. It was wet and sticky. They'd hit her with something.

Defeated, she relaxed her body.

A cell phone rang out. Allison jerked as the noise awakened her nerves.

"Yeah, it's me."

That accent. She'd heard it before.

"Naw, we ain't doing that. We don't take orders from you. Besides, I ain't killin' her. I already told you that I need my job at the tire shop."

Well, if he wasn't going to kill her, then she'd take her chances on getting away.

The blows to his head still had him a little shaky. He managed to stand and took a few small steps to give his legs a try before setting off to find her. He picked up the flashlight and went into the bedroom to see if they'd left anything behind that might help.

His heart sank to think they'd taken her again. If she was dead, they would have left her here. Now wasn't the time to think about it. His mind felt hazy and he knew he needed to be coherent enough to drive. Jackson headed out to the front yard and pulled out his cell phone. He opened the app that tracked the GPS device he'd given her.

Fifteen minutes later, he arrived at an abandoned, half-burnt farmhouse. Behind it stood a dilapidated barn. The roof sagged and bowed like a rotten tree. He turned onto a nearby gravel road and parked. Under the cover of darkness, he crept toward the old barn. His head still ached. As he got closer, he noticed a Stonewater police car parked in front of the barn. He eased around the side of the barn and slid against the back wall. Light shone through the old boards. Jackson closed one eye and watched through the wide crack. Dim camping lanterns created enough illumination for him to see what was going on.

Jackson moved down the wall a few inches to look through another wide gap.

There she was.

Allison was lying on a straw-covered floor in the sweats he'd bought her. They were covered in dirt, but he didn't notice any blood on them. She had to be terrified. He wished he could signal to her so she would know he was there.

She must be furious with him. Not that he could blame her. It wasn't easy admitting that he'd let her slip away from him. Not once, but twice. Whoever they were dealing with, these guys weren't amateurs. But it wasn't by accident that they hadn't killed him back at the house. Whoever was doing this didn't want him dead; they only wanted Allison. That thought sent chills through him. The urge to pray for her overwhelmed him. Praying wasn't something he was good at anymore, but he had to pray for her.

God, forgive me for the years I've neglected to talk to You. I just need You to help me save Allison. I can't let her die. Give me the wisdom and courage to get her out of there. Amen.

A sense of peace washed over him. It had been a long time since he'd prayed. He could only hope God would hear his prayers this time.

A man's voice sounded from the corner of the barn. Jackson stilled his breathing, hoping to hear what he was saying, and closed his eyes for a few seconds to refocus his vision in the darkness. The voice sounded very familiar, but he couldn't remember where he'd heard it before. He opened his eyes and stared through the hole. The man donned a cowboy hat and appeared to be talking on a cell phone. Jackson wished he could hear the conversation, but the man hung up after a few seconds.

Allison shifted her body on the floor. A different man emerged from the shadows. This one was shorter and more muscular than the guy on the phone. Tattoos covered the left side of his face, making it obvious he had gang affiliations. Although this wasn't the man from the highway, he seemed just as dangerous.

"Hey, coward!"

"Who are you calling *coward*?" the man in the hat yelled back.

Jackson could hear both men barking at each other. This time, the words were clear. There was an obvious breakdown in the camaraderie. Jackson hoped this could work to his advantage.

"I ain't going to prison for killing nobody. I already told y'all I gotta be here to take care of my kid. Besides, y'all can't trust nobody to run that tire shop like I do. The boss said he wants to talk to her before you kill her. Don't go getting any wild ideas."

"The boss told you that?"

"Uh-huh. Here." He shoved the phone at the other man.

Jackson couldn't believe what he was hearing. Something wasn't making sense. Why would they want her alive after they'd tried to kill her several times?

The other man swatted at the phone. It fell to the floor with a heavy thud.

Allison moved again on the floor. Jackson watched as she struggled to lean against the barn wall. He had to get to her. The only way he could break her out of there was if he found a way to break in. One way or another, he would get to her.

And if he had to give his life for hers, then so be it.

Allison listened to the men argue. It was like watching two little boys fight over a toy. One of them didn't have the stomach for murder. That was the only thing that had played in her favor so far.

Memories flashed in her mind like lightning. The cowboy. It was him! It was Tex from the truck. She closed her eyes and tried to remember the details. It was a night she wanted to forget but couldn't. Tex had yelled out that he wasn't going to hurt her. But the man who'd tried to kill her wasn't here. She was sure of it. His was a face she couldn't forget.

Pain shot through her head as her hair was yanked backward.

"Look at this picture." The tattooed man's breath hit her face.

Allison moaned in pain as she forced herself to focus through the tears swelling in her eyes.

"Do you know this man?"

"No."

Another yank sent more pain screaming through her head.

"Look again."

This time she pretended to study it.

"No!" She screamed back to make sure they heard her. But she did recognize him. He was the man in the hospital who'd tried to kill her. It was the man who'd held her down and given her the shot. Why was it so important that she knew who he was?

The hand on her head let go, and the two men walked away, leaving her on the floor. The thought of Jackson sent stabbing pains through her chest. Right now, she couldn't think that he might be dead. It hurt too much to have those thoughts. The only thing she needed to focus on was escaping and staying alive. It was up to her whether or not she lived or died.

She waited until both men were far enough away to pull herself up into a sitting position. She remained motionless as she studied the perimeter of the barn. It was cold and damp, and it looked as if it had been abandoned for the past fifty years. A few old gardening tools and a saw blade hung from nails on the wall near the front door. If only she could get to them, she would at least have a weapon.

Allison looked behind her and caught a glimpse of

something moving on the other side of the wall. Her chest tightened. She huffed out a few ragged breaths as her hopes ran wild. It might be a long shot to believe it was Jackson out there, but it was all the hope she had. She eased her back against the wall and turned her face toward a crack so she could hear.

"Allison." A whisper sounded into her ear.

It was Jackson! He'd come for her.

He continued to whisper. "Don't talk, just listen. I'm going to get you out of there, but I need you to work with me."

Allison adjusted her head to show a small nod. She didn't dare utter a word.

"Good girl. You have to wait for my signal."

She wanted to believe with all her heart that Jackson would get her out alive, but she'd be a fool if she thought it was easy. There was a big chance this could go wrong.

"El Capitán, why do you come here?"

A man in a police officer's uniform appeared where the other two stood. "I have to make sure you morons aren't messing this up for me. I know if I want something done right, I have to do it myself. Mauricio proved that."

"She don't know what she's done wrong." Tex spat chewing tobacco at the cop's feet.

The cop moved back a couple of steps and glared at Tex. "Oh, yeah? Well, you let me be the judge of that."

"Speaking of being the judge." The tattooed man wagged a finger in the officer's face. "You have made El Verdugo angry. He is tired of you trying to take credit for his hard work. You have forgotten how to take orders. That badge does not make you his boss." He obviously didn't like this cop.

She couldn't believe what she was hearing. Jackson had been right all along. But who was this El Capitán? Did Jackson know him? Whoever he was, she was sure he had no problem killing someone. Or telling someone to do it for him. He walked over to where she sat on the barn floor. His boots were shined to perfection, his uniform pressed and smooth.

He knelt and shoved a cell phone into her face. "Do you know this man?"

Allison glanced at him and then back at the phone. This time it was a picture of a man with rough features, a long greasy ponytail, a tattoo of a woman on his neck and the eyes of a killer. It was a mug shot. He obviously had friends in high places, because someone like that shouldn't be allowed to roam free.

"I don't know him."

He grabbed her face with his other hand. "Let's try this again. Have you seen this man?"

She stared at the phone.

"I've seen him." Pain shot through her cheek as he gripped harder.

"Ah, so now we're getting somewhere." He put the phone back into his pocket and released her. "What about the woman in the truck?"

Allison shook her head. "I didn't see a woman."

The cop paced around where she lay on the floor. He scratched at the stubble on his chin. "Okay. What did you see?"

Allison swallowed. "Nothing."

The cop bent over and stared into Allison's eyes. "You should've stayed in Houston where you belong. You almost ruined everything." He stood up and turned to the man with the tattoos. "Shoot her."

Fear shook her. The name tag on his uniform read *Schmille*. Jackson was right.

"We don't take orders from you." The shorter man aimed a gun at the cop.

"Yup, that's right. Carlos Vega Calderón will be here any minute. That's who we take orders from. Besides, he already told us not to kill her. Said she's worth some money. Guess he has other plans for her." Tex grinned at Schmille.

Allison's stomach lurched. She had to figure a way out of here. She'd rather die than be held captive by the cartel. It wasn't a secret what they were planning on doing to her. She closed her eyes and began to pray. When she finished, she looked around the barn to find the men huddled together at the front door. No one was looking in her direction. This was it. She needed to take her chance.

Allison leaned against the wall and listened for Jackson. She didn't hear him.

"Jackson." She made sure to keep her voice down so they wouldn't hear her.

There was no reply. The men were still talking at the door of the barn. She couldn't wait another second. There had to be a way out without them seeing her. It was a risky chance, but she had to take it.

Jackson's finger itched to pull the trigger as he lined his sight on Schmille. It was him. The egotistical pain in his side who thought he was superior to everyone on the force. And to top it off, he was working with Calderón, one of the biggest drug kingpins in Texas. Or El Verdugo, the Executioner, as they called him on the streets. No wonder they were trying to kill Allison. She'd foiled their plans to dispose of the DEA agent.

Someone had blown the agent's cover. And now it was obvious who did it.

Schmille had to be the one tipping them off the entire time. Jackson wished he could call Devon to tell him what was happening. He wondered if the DEA had more agents undercover working on this case? He also wondered how many Stonewater police officers were going to go down with Schmille.

Right now, he had to concentrate on how to get Allison out of there. He needed to find a way to get in without them noticing. As he moved to make his way to the edge of the barn, something rustled behind him.

"Don't take another step."

Jackson stopped and raised both hands in the air. His adrenaline revved up as his brain scrambled to figure out an escape without getting shot.

"Drop the gun."

Jackson did as he was told and let the pistol fall to the ground on a pile of dead leaves.

"Now take the one from your ankle holster and kick it away, too."

Smart move. This guy had to be another dirty cop. He put his backup weapon on the ground and kicked it away.

"Turn around real slow. I won't hesitate to shoot you, so don't act stupid."

Jackson turned around. It was one of the men from inside the barn. Jackson searched his face. As far as Jackson knew, he'd never met this man before.

"Who do you work for?" Jackson's gut told him it wasn't the cartel. If it was, he'd already be dead.

The man kept his .35 mm aimed at Jackson's forehead. "You first."

The two of them glared at each other, neither wanting to flinch. Jackson wondered what happened to the man's thick Texas drawl. It wasn't there now. In fact, there was hardly a detectable accent at all.

The man repeated his question. "I'm going to try this one more time. Who do you work for?"

"Myself." It wasn't a total lie. He wasn't there in a police capacity. He was only there to save Allison.

The man inched closer and started to pat Jackson down with one hand while keeping his gun trained on him with the other. He pulled Jackson's badge from his hip pocket and threw it onto the ground.

"Start talking."

"What's there to say? Now you know who I work for. What are you going to do?"

"What are you doing out here by yourself?" The man moved back and put his gun down to his side. "You're Archer, right?"

Jackson felt better now that the gun wasn't aimed at him. He might as well tell the truth. He wasn't totally sure he could trust him, but the fact that he was still alive gave him a little more faith in this guy.

"Yeah, and I'm here for her."

A voice sounded from the side of the barn. "Hey! What's taking you so long out there?"

The man frowned and put a finger up to signal for Jackson to stay quiet. "It must be that food we ate! I'm feelin' sicker than an alligator in a vegetable stand!"

The man shrugged his shoulders as Jackson grinned at him.

He leaned forward and whispered. "Hey, I'm not

even from Texas. I'm from Wisconsin." He picked up Jackson's weapons and badge and handed them back to him.

"How'd you know I was out here?" Jackson was relieved that no one else had seen him.

"I assumed you would come after her." He walked toward a grove of mesquite trees behind the barn. "Come on, follow me. We can't risk them overhearing us."

Jackson looked back toward the barn.

"Don't worry. They won't kill her."

"How do you know that?"

"Because that's my job."

Jackson stopped walking. "Did you kill that DEA agent?"

The man halted in his tracks. He didn't turn around. "She was my friend. I'm here for the same reason you are, only I was too late."

Jackson didn't need any further explanation.

"I'm sorry. It was terrible what they did to her."

The man turned around. "We need to stay focused if we're going to get your girl out of there."

Jackson couldn't agree more. "Are you the one who broke into my parents' house?"

"Yes. And before you get upset, I didn't hit her over the head. I wasn't the only one in the house. I did what I could to make sure you both weren't killed."

"Who are you and what agency are you working with?" Jackson wanted to trust him.

"Look, I shouldn't have blown my cover, not even for your friend. Just know I'm on your side. Nothing will happen to her if you don't blow my cover in there, but I'm going to need your help."

Jackson had one more question that he couldn't wait

to get an answer to. "What do you know about that cop in there?" He tilted his head toward the barn.

The man shot him an irritated glance. "First, tell me something. What do *you* know about that cop in there? He's from your department."

"Dirty." Jackson wasn't going to comment more on the subject. The less he said about Schmille, the better. Right now, all he wanted was to get Allison out of there. "What's your plan for the girl?"

He watched the man pull the cowboy hat from his head, rake a hand through his hair, then shove the hat back on. His features hardened as he contemplated his next words.

"I'm going to need your help."

"How can I trust you? How do I know you're not working with the cartel, too?"

"Looks like you know more about Schmille than you're letting on."

"So do you." Jackson shot back. "What do you need my help with?"

"You're coming back in there with me."

"That's suicide, man. No way. You bring Allison out here to me and I'll get her to safety. Why would you need me to go in there? What kind of half-baked plan is this?"

The agent's irritation surfaced. "Do you know how hard we've worked to take this cartel down? They killed one of our agents, and I'm not about to blow this. I need you on the inside with me. This is going down my way. Tonight. If you want me to protect her, then you have to trust me."

Jackson paced in front of him. So this guy was with

the DEA. "Schmille will kill me the minute I walk in there."

"No, he won't."

"How can you be so sure?" Jackson didn't believe any of this. What was the DEA up to? He wasn't about to put Allison's life on the line. Again.

"We want the head of the snake. That's who Schmille takes his orders from. All I have to do is tell Schmille that we were told not to shoot you until we get the go-ahead. Look, I already have enough evidence to take down Schmille. We could've done that a long time ago. Schmille is a tiny fish. We want the shark."

Jackson nodded. "All right. Let's do this, then."

SIXTEEN

Pain radiated from her legs as she tried to stretch them. She rubbed her eyes to focus in the dimly lit barn. The men were still talking with their backs to her.

She whispered to Jackson through the wall. "Are you still out there?"

He didn't answer.

The group of men turned and walked back toward the center of the barn. Allison heard angry shouting from a few of them.

"Look at what I found in the woods, y'all."

Her plan for escaping vanished like a whisper of smoke. It was over now. The only person who could get her out was now in this with her. She wanted to run to Jackson, but for both of their sakes she stayed silent.

Schmille turned and glared at Jackson. "Kill him! Now."

Tex shook his head. "Uh-uh." He wagged a finger at Schmille. "No, no. You don't get to tell us what to do. El Verdugo will be here soon. We only take orders from him."

It relieved Allison to hear that Schmille had no authority with these people, but the threat of someone named El Verdugo didn't sound good. Anyone who they called the Executioner wasn't about to let them walk out of here alive. This was it. She needed to face reality. They weren't ever getting out of here. They were going to die.

Jackson's eyes met hers. He mouthed something but she couldn't make it out. She was too afraid to respond.

"I'm gonna put him over there with the girl. That way we can keep an eye on them." Tex shoved Jackson while he kept a gun pressed into his back.

"Here." Schmille tossed Tex a pair of handcuffs. "Put these on him."

Tex clicked the cuffs into place on Jackson's wrists, then pushed him onto the ground with more force than was necessary. Allison inched her way closer to Jackson.

He shot her an angry glare. "Don't talk to me."

The fury in his voice shocked her. She did as she was told, but she resented the fact that he was being so harsh with her.

Allison scooted a few inches away from Jackson as he stared at the ground. She wondered why they hadn't shot him when they found him outside. There had to be some reason why Tex didn't kill him.

If Schmille was working with the cartel, who was Tex working for? Was Jackson in this somehow, too? Something wasn't right. In fact, nothing was making sense.

She stole a glance at Jackson. Could he be in this with them somehow? If that was true, then he had no reason to keep her alive. Allison leaned against the wall. It didn't matter if it made sense or not. Any hope she had of making it out alive had already disappeared.

* * *

The urge to pull her close made his body ache. There was nothing he wanted more in that moment than to hold her and tell her to trust him. He'd come off as angry, but he knew he had to. It was the only way he could make sure she kept her emotions in check. For now, he had to keep from looking at Allison, because the eyes don't lie. He knew those men would see right through him if he looked at her.

Schmille walked over and kicked Jackson's boot. "Thought you were so smart, didn't you?"

Jackson didn't respond. He stared at the floor, refusing to give Schmille the satisfaction of making him mad.

"What's the matter, boy? You surprised to see me here?"

Jackson kept his gaze fixed on the floor. "Nope."

Laughter erupted. "You know how much fun it's been for me the past five years? Watching you become less and less of a man. Less of a cop. Wallowing in grief until you gave up on everything. I hoped you'd just fade away into oblivion and be none the wiser, but you had to go play the rescuer. I guess since you couldn't save your wife and kid, you thought you'd save her." Schmille kicked Allison's foot.

Silence filled the room as every head turned in his direction. He heard Allison say his name, but he couldn't acknowledge her. Anger swelled deep inside and his body shook from the explosion of emotions rising within him. He glared at Schmille. "Hey, Captain. There's something I need to tell you." He whispered so the man would have to bend down to hear him. "Come closer."

"It won't matter now, boy. You're as good as dead." Schmille bent over, laughing at his own sick joke. Jackson tilted his head back, then slammed it into Schmille's face, sending him stumbling backward. He wiped at his mouth with the back of his hand. Blood trickled from his nose.

"Don't ever talk about my wife and kid again." Jackson trembled with anger.

"You're a dead man now, Archer!" Schmille wiped the blood with the back of his hand.

The agent stepped between them with both arms raised in the air. "Hold on, fellas. We don't have time for this. Mr. Calderón and his men will be here any minute. He might take a notion to shoot all of us if he sees this chaos. We need to get this deal finished and then you two can kill each other."

Schmille shoved the agent as he walked past him. He turned and pointed at Jackson, then at Allison. "They're mine. After we pick up this shipment, those two belong to me."

"How do you plan to pull that off?" One of the other cartel members spoke up.

Jackson hadn't heard this guy say a word. He wondered who this man worked for. He was either cartel or law enforcement, but at this point it was hard to tell the good guys from the bad. The man answered his own question. "You can't pull it off. And you know why?"

Schmille snarled at him. "You don't know anything."

"Because then I kill *you*." The man's tone was ice-cold. It was clear he wasn't playing games.

"You go ahead, but not before I kill them." Schmille pointed at Allison. "She's first." He wiped his mouth again. "You had to go sticking your nose where it didn't belong." Anger flashed in his eyes. He drew his weapon and aimed it at Allison's head. "This is ridiculous. I see no reason to keep you alive."

Jackson felt Allison's body stiffen next to him. He leaned in front of her and stared Rusty Schmille in his hateful eyes.

Laughter echoed through the barn. "Archer, you're only making this easier for me. Neither of you are walking out of here. Might as well get me a two-for-one out of the deal."

Jackson heard a whimper coming from Allison. He needed her to stay quiet. "Don't say anything," he muttered between clenched teeth. "This will be over soon."

The agent interrupted. "Come on, let's all calm down and wait for Calderón." He motioned for Schmille and the other man to go with him back to the front of the barn.

Jackson was thankful for a quiet moment to talk to Allison. As soon as they were all out of sight, he leaned over to whisper in her ear. The feel of her hair against his face sent waves of tingles down his back. Her skin smelled of body spray and an unmistakable scent of hay.

"Don't talk, Allison. Just listen. There are undercover DEA agents in here with us. I can't tell you who they are. I'm not sure how this is going to play out, but you have to believe that no one is going to hurt you."

"It's Tex, isn't it?"

"Tex?"

"Yeah, the one in the cowboy hat. The one with the thick Texas accent."

Jackson grinned. She was smarter than he'd given her credit for. "Doesn't matter. Just stay quiet and let this play out. It will all be over soon." Jackson rubbed his nose against her ear. "And when it is, I'd like to take you to dinner."

She pressed her head into his and nodded. "I would love that," she whispered.

A truck roared up to the barn. Jackson pulled away from Allison to put a couple of inches between them. "Remember, don't talk to them. And be ready for anything. Just watch my cues. I'll let you know what to do."

It had to be Calderón, the so-called head of the snake. He wondered what the DEA planned to do in order to take this guy down. After several slams from car doors, all the men entered the barn.

"What do we have here?" A tall, slender man wearing too much gold jewelry walked in.

Schmille spoke up first. "I'd like to help dispose of them for you, if you'd let me."

Calderón waved a hand in the air. "Get away from me. I was talking about the shipment. Where are my weapons? I have a plane leaving for Guatemala." He walked over to Allison and kneeled, putting his face inches from hers.

Jackson made eye contact with the agent and thought he saw a hint of uneasiness. He prayed Calderón didn't put a hand on Allison. There wasn't much he could do about it with handcuffs on.

"Do you know why you're here?"

Allison shook her head as fear cloaked her face.

"You ran my brother off the road, and you took his picture to turn him in. My brother is Mauricio Vega Calderón." The man's tone was flat and emotionless.

Tears sprang to her eyes and Jackson feared the inevitable. Her spirit was too sweet to deal with this kind of evil. She was going to break.

"I tried to help him." Allison shook her head in denial. "He shot at me. I called for help. I wanted to help him."

"By taking his picture and turning it over to the police?" It was more a statement than a question.

"He tried to…"

Jackson kicked her foot to keep her from saying another word.

Schmille interrupted. "Calderón, we need to get this show on the road. I don't have all night. Let's get this shipment inspected. We also need the drug shipment so we can get it back to the tire shop. Besides, I already told you, I'll take care of those two. No one will ever find them."

Schmille walked out of the barn without waiting for a response from Calderón. After Calderón headed outside, the others followed. Jackson studied every man as they left the room. He could feel the raw tension. Minutes passed, but none of them came back.

Jackson remembered a couple of loose boards while he was hiding behind the barn. He'd pried a few open hoping to allow Allison an escape. He slid around Allison's back and pushed them with the toe of his boot. One fell to the ground outside. He pushed another, and then another until there was a gap wide enough for them to fit through.

"We need to get out of here now." Jackson hoisted himself up and waited for Allison to pull herself from the ground. "Follow me and be quiet."

Jackson turned sideways and slithered through the crack. As he slipped through the crack, Schmille and Calderón saw him. Schmille reached for his gun. Jackson sank to the ground and pulled Allison through the crack with him. Bullets hit the wall where they'd been sitting only seconds before.

The sound of commotion filled the night air. Jackson peered through the boards. He turned to her. "Come on."

He scanned the area for a safe place to go. "This way." They headed for a thick grove of trees. Once far enough away, he stopped and sat on a large rock.

Allison sat next to him, panting to catch her breath. "What do we do now? We can't go any farther with your hands behind your back."

The cold breeze stung as he inhaled large gulps of air to steady his breathing. "I have a key in my coat pocket. See if you can get it out."

Allison reached into the right pocket of his jacket and pulled the key out.

"I never asked you how you escaped the truck that night."

She smiled up at him. "I took a survival training class. I learned how to break free if someone zip-ties your hands together. Too bad you're not tied with plastic. I could show you how to get out."

"I'm speechless. I didn't know you could do something like that." He liked her resiliency. If he had to be honest, there wasn't much he didn't like about Allison Moore.

"Let me get those cuffs unlocked so we can get moving." She fumbled through the different keys on the key ring and looked up at him.

"It's the small key next to my truck key."

"Got it."

He turned around so she could unlock the cuffs. She

handed him the keys and the cuffs, and he shoved them into his pocket.

Jackson smiled. "That's my girl. Now let's get out of here." He grabbed her hand and turned to run. He didn't know when he'd started thinking of her as *his* girl, but he liked the way it sounded. Jackson flinched as a tree branch snapped.

Gunfire exploded behind them.

Allison's heart skidded to a stop. Fear paralyzed her. It took her a second to determine if she'd been shot. Jackson pulled her into his arms and held her tight.

"Don't move," he whispered. "They're right behind us. We won't get far if we run."

"Well, well. I guess you two lovebirds thought you could get away."

Rusty Schmille pointed a gun at both of them.

"How'd you get out of there alive?" Jackson's tone was blunt.

"I knew you'd run. I wasn't about to let you get away with her."

Schmille paced in front of them as if he were trying to figure out his next move. She didn't know how this would play out, but she worried that it would not go in their favor. Not with a gun pointed at them. She was almost sure Jackson didn't have a weapon on him. It didn't seem likely that they would've allowed him to keep one if they were taking him as a hostage. Allison noticed Jackson keeping a steady eye on Schmille.

"I've been doing my job better than you think I have, Captain."

"Really? I doubt that, Archer. You can't do your job

any better now than you could five years ago. You're still wallowing in grief like a pathetic loser."

Allison felt Jackson's body stiffen. She didn't know what Schmille was getting at, but it was enough to throw Jackson off.

Schmille grabbed her and pulled her to him. He wrapped an arm around her neck and shoved the end of his pistol into her temple. Tears formed in her eyes as the realization set in that this was it for her.

"Let her go!" Jackson's voice echoed through the trees.

Schmille mocked him by laughing. "I want to play a little game first. I want to see the look on your face when you find out what a fool you've been. You were so full of yourself before your wife died. You and Devon acted like you could run that department all by yourselves. You never did warm up to me being your superior."

"Don't do this, Rusty. Let's talk this out."

Allison couldn't figure out what he was up to. Jackson wasn't one to back down without a fight. She'd just met him, but she knew him better than that.

"Talk? I don't think so. There's nothing to talk about. I can't let you both walk away from here knowing I work with the cartel."

Jackson shook his head. "The DEA already knows about you, Schmille. It's always a shame when a cop goes bad. You just couldn't resist the temptation of seeing all that money and not being able to have any of it for yourself. You got greedy."

The grip around Allison's neck grew tighter as he pressed the gun harder against her head.

"Greed? It had nothing to do with greed." Schmille

removed the gun from her head and pointed it at Jackson.

Jackson put his hands into the air. "If you say so."

He turned the gun back on Allison and pressed it into her temple. "I think I'm getting a little tired of this game. Let's say I kill her first, then you." Schmille slid the gun down the side of her face to her cheek. "Such a shame to kill another woman that you love."

Allison's mouth fell open. It felt as if the ground had fallen away from under their feet. Jackson's face blanched and he stumbled backward. He grabbed onto a tree to steady his balance. Grief washed over his face, then changed into something else. Fury filled his eyes.

They were looking into the face of Hope and Natalie's killer.

Jackson's hands trembled as rage boiled to the surface. After all these years, he had his answer. What he didn't know was why. In that moment, however, *why* didn't seem to matter. He couldn't save them, but he could save Allison.

"Behind you!" Jackson yelled.

Schmille's eyes darted around to see what was coming. Jackson lunged at Schmille, knocking him to the ground. Schmille's gun flew from his hand and landed in a pile of leaves and sticks.

Jackson tumbled across the ground and pinned the man beneath him. As he drew back a fist, the sound of gunfire caused his arm to freeze in midair. Allison stood over them holding Schmille's pistol.

"She doesn't have the guts." Schmille scoffed at her.

Jackson glanced at Allison. "Don't be so sure."

"Do it then!" Panic shook Schmille's voice.

"Don't do it, Allison." Jackson turned back to Schmille. "I think I'll let them take you in. Prison is a tough place for dirty cops."

"If I go, you're going with me."

Jackson couldn't believe what he was hearing. "You're insane."

"You'll go for attempted murder."

"I didn't try to kill anyone. Yet."

Schmille snickered. "You will. I'm the one who killed your wife, Archer. It was me. And now I'm going to tell you how I did it."

Anger burned through his body like lightning. Schmille rolled and threw Jackson off him. He raced toward Allison, but Jackson scrambled up and lunged at him. Both men fell to the ground. Jackson was fighting in a blind rage as he swung and landed a fist on Schmille's jaw.

Jackson pinned Schmille down again, then pulled his pistol from his waistband and pointed it at the dirty cop's head. His hand shook as he fought the urge to kill him.

"Jackson, no!" Allison's voice echoed through the trees.

"Explain! Tell me how you killed my family!" Anger raged through his veins.

Schmille grinned at him. Jackson landed another blow on the man's face. Blood covered his lips as he spoke. "She came to the tire shop to get her tire fixed. You're the one who sent her there, remember? She was spoiled and entitled. A beautiful little rich girl."

Jackson raised a hand to hit him again. Schmille's eyes closed as he braced for it.

"Jackson." Allison's soft voice pleaded with him.

He lowered his arm and sucked in a ragged breath. He had to know the truth. It was going to hurt, and it would haunt him for the rest of his life, but he had to know.

"What did you do? Tell me what you did to them?"

Schmille laughed again and lifted a hand to wipe the blood from his lips. "She came inside the office because she was in a hurry. She caught me making a drop-off. I could see it in her eyes that she knew what she'd witnessed, and she was heading straight to you with that information." He shrugged. "So I waited for her to leave, and then I followed her. Once we got to the bend in the road, I pulled up next to her and ran her off into the ravine."

The world around Jackson grew hazy. Years of anger and grief melded together deep inside, ready to explode their way out. The urge to get even robbed him of his senses. Jackson's body shook. He stood and backed away, keeping his gun trained on Schmille's head.

"You left them there to die."

Schmille laughed like an evil villain. "I wondered when you were going to come find me. Kill them both and dispose of the bodies."

Jackson spun around to find the DEA agent with a gun pointing right at Allison's head. Jackson turned his gun on the agent.

"Drop it, man. Don't make a move, or I'll kill you." Jackson's voice shook.

The agent stared him in the eyes, then turned back to Allison. "Drop the weapon, ma'am."

"Do it, Allison." Jackson kept his gun on the agent.

Allison bent down and gently placed the weapon on the ground.

The agent kept his gun on her. "Move over there with him." He motioned for her to stand with Jackson.

Allison shuffled her feet across the rocks and slid next to him. He wrapped an arm around her and pulled her close. Her body shook against him.

Schmille scrambled off the ground and grabbed his pistol, aiming it at Jackson. "Archer, you're a terrible cop."

SEVENTEEN

Allison hid her face into Jackson's shoulder. She didn't want to acknowledge the fact that they were going to die right here. As afraid as she was, she couldn't help but think about Jackson's pain. To find out what had happened to his wife and child like this must feel as bad as dying.

Schmille yanked Allison from Jackson's grip and pulled hair back. He shoved the tip of his gun under her chin. "I think I'll kill her myself. I want Archer to see it this time."

Allison closed her eyes and began to pray. It wasn't dying that she was afraid of. In that moment, she was more afraid for Jackson. The seconds that Schmille held his gun under her chin felt more like minutes. She braced for the inevitable as she ached to tell Jackson that she loved him and didn't blame him for anything. Allison closed her eyes and waited.

"Drop the gun! Drop it now."

"What are you doing, you idiot?" Schmille sounded shocked.

"Let her go."

Allison recognized Tex's voice.

"Well, well. You mean all along you were working with the DEA?"

Allison opened her eyes. Schmille looked both angry and horrified.

"I'm not going to say it again. Let her go." Tex took a step toward them.

"I guess that agent was a real good friend of yours, wasn't she?" Schmille grinned. "Shame what they did to her." He pressed the gun harder against Allison's temple.

Schmille's hand jerked as a shot rang out.

Allison felt her body sink to the ground. Seconds later, Jackson scooped her into his arms and held her to his chest.

"You're okay. You're safe now."

She took a deep breath and blinked. "What happened?"

"I think you fainted when you heard the gun go off."

"I'm not dead?" She felt her chin. "I didn't get shot?"

"No, you're not dead." Jackson smiled, then brushed his lips across hers. He smoothed her hair from her face.

"Then who fired the gun?" She struggled to sit up.

Jackson helped her to her feet. The DEA agent stood over Schmille's lifeless body. It was over. Memories flooded Allison's head as she studied the other man holding a gun. Tex was really one of the good guys all along.

He shoved his gun into the holster under his shirt. "I'm an undercover DEA agent. They sent me to expose Rusty Schmille and the cartel he was working for."

Allison turned to Jackson. "It was true?"

Jackson nodded. "Yes, he's telling the truth. Schmille was the dirty cop."

"I'm Agent Ross Lorenzo." He stuck out a hand.

She still had so many questions. She shook his hand as she looked from the agent to Jackson. "But…you're Tex." She had no idea he was working undercover. "I'm so sorry I didn't listen when you said you weren't going to hurt me. I had no way of knowing. I mean, you were with the man who tried to kill me, so I didn't know what else to think."

"Well, I wasn't expecting you to pull a gun on me. Mauricio, the man who was with me, would've killed you if I hadn't let you go. Cartels aren't forgiving."

Allison nodded. "I'm positive he would've."

"I was trying to get you to safety just like Jackson was. He wasn't even aware of our plans. We didn't know how many dirty cops Schmille had on the force working with him. The fewer people who knew about us, the safer we were."

"This still isn't making sense to me." Allison stared at Schmille lying on the ground, then turned to Jackson. "Does this make sense to you?"

Allison looked down to see Jackson still holding a gun in his hand. He shoved it into his waistband.

"Yeah, it does now."

Allison turned back to the agent. "But the man who tried to kill me was with you. Why?"

"Right, I know. I was arranging for an agent to get you to a safe house without him knowing it. I had to make Schmille think I was still working with him. If he had realized I was with the DEA, he would've killed me on the spot. It sounds complicated, but I had more than one objective. Take them down and keep you safe."

Jackson interjected. "Schmille was a terrible cop. He lost his training when he lost his integrity. He was so far gone he didn't know how to be anything more than a criminal. That's why he finally got caught."

"What did Schmille actually do?" Allison glanced at his lifeless face, then turned away.

Jackson spoke first. "Schmille was working with the cartel. He was selling drugs out of the tire shop in town. Our department did business with them for our vehicles. The cartel was using Schmille to keep the heat off the tire shop so they could sell the drugs."

The agent interrupted. "Not to mention laundering the money. He also acted as an informant for the cartel. They were shipping illegal weapons out of the tire shop, too. I'm here because the cartel killed one of our agents. She was the woman in the truck that you ran off the road. Schmille knew she was an undercover agent because we told him. We usually try to work closely with the local agencies. But he tipped off the cartel and they had her killed. At the time, no one knew it was Schmille who was dirty. The DEA sent me in undercover. This time we didn't tell anyone so Schmille didn't know who I was."

"Doesn't it take a long time to work your way into the cartel?" Allison didn't know much about the cartel, but she'd watched a few things on the news.

The agent grinned. "Smart girl. Yes, it does. We had some undercover guys working within the same cartel. They were trusted and had been for a while. I was trusted because they were trusted. No one was the wiser. In fact, Schmille didn't know I was working on the inside to take him and the cartel down."

The agent turned to Jackson. "I'm sorry, man. I didn't know he'd killed your family. None of us had any idea about that. We'll open an investigation and get everyone responsible."

"Thanks, man."

Allison noticed tears in Jackson's eyes. She turned away to hide her own.

"I still can't believe we got Calderón. This has been a long time coming. Hey, do you guys need a ride somewhere? I can get someone to take you home. I'm going to be out here for quite a while. Agents were going to move in right after they made the drop-off. Calderón should be in custody by now, but there's a lot of work left to do."

"No, my truck is parked about a half mile up the road. We'll be fine."

The two men shook hands. Allison watched the agent walk back to the barn where a frenzy of law enforcement officers and SWAT teams swarmed.

"Now what?" Allison waited for Jackson to tell her it was time for her to head back to Houston. It was something she'd wanted to do since this whole mess had started. But now, she didn't know what she wanted.

He grabbed her hand and started walking.

"Let's go see Devon."

They rode to the hospital in complete silence. The sun peeked over the horizon and turned the night sky a beautiful shade of orange. Allison's head rested on the back of the seat. Jackson stole occasional glances at her and noticed her dozing off. As hard as he tried to find the words to tell her what he was feeling, he couldn't bring himself to say them.

A sigh left her lips, and she raised a hand to brush away the hair tickling her face. She was still wearing the sweat suit he'd bought her along with the slippers. He grinned as he remembered how he'd stood in the dollar store debating on the right size. The slippers were tattered and ripped, her clothes were dingy, and her left cheek had a streak of dirt on it. Even in the worst conditions, she still looked beautiful.

Out of nowhere, pain shot through his heart as Schmille's words flooded his memory. It hurt him so much to know that there was nothing he could've done for Hope and Natalie, or his unborn son. But somehow knowing the truth gave him a sense of peace that he hadn't felt in five years.

Allison lifted her head and looked around.

"Are we there?"

"A few more minutes."

"I didn't mean to doze off. I feel like I could sleep for years now that this is over. It will feel good to be home and in my own bed again." She bolted up and stared at him. "I just remembered my car isn't drivable." She slumped back down in the seat with a look of defeat on her face.

"I'll take you back to Houston if you need me to." He smiled even though the thought of her leaving wasn't something that made him feel like smiling.

"Oh, I couldn't ask you to do that. I'll get Maddie and Scott to take me home. I've put you through enough as it is."

Jackson nodded. It was obvious she was looking for reasons to get away from him and go back to her normal life. Not that he blamed her. He'd dragged her through some horrible things trying to save her. Looking back, maybe he would've done things a lot differently.

"Jackson."

"Yeah?"

"Do you think we'll ever see each other again after today?"

A lump formed in his throat. After all these years, he hadn't thought he was ready to move on. Now, looking at her sitting next to him, he couldn't think of anything else other than a life with her in it.

"Sure, we will."

Allison smiled, then turned to look out the window. They rode in silence until they reached the hospital. Jackson parked and they made their way to Devon's room.

Jackson remembered the night he came to see Allison in the hospital. He'd held her hand as the doctor stitched her knee. He couldn't have guessed their lives would become so entangled.

Jackson knocked on Devon's door before opening it and walking in.

"Hey, guys." Devon sat up and grinned at them.

The sight of his old friend in the hospital was more than he could bear. Jackson walked over and hugged him. Tears burned his eyes. He'd fought back tears since he'd first heard about Devon, but now in the safety of his friend's room, he knew he could let it all go. After a few seconds, they broke their embrace and wiped at their eyes.

Devon laughed. "I'm not crying, you're crying."

Jackson shook his head and turned to Devon's wife. "Karen, I don't know how you deal with this guy."

She reached to grab a tissue from the bedside table. "I don't know, either. It's good to see you, Jackson." She turned to Allison. "I'm Devon's wife. Would you like to come with me to get some coffee?"

Allison wiped her cheeks and smiled. Jackson waited until they left the room to tell Devon the whole story.

"How'd you get shot, man? Do you know how bad I felt leaving you back there?" Jackson sank down in the recliner by Devon's bed.

"I was headed to the station after I dropped you and Allison off at your house. This car comes out of nowhere. I don't know how they knew I was in Richard Maber's truck. The department will have to replace it now. His truck is riddled with bullet holes."

"I guarantee it was Schmille. I don't know how you survived."

Devon nodded in agreement. "They had eyes everywhere. It makes me wonder how many dirty cops we really had."

Jackson suspected a couple of them. "I think the rookie was one of them. I haven't heard anything official yet."

"The smug rookie, huh? He wasn't a cop. He was a kid on an ego trip. Rusty, on the other hand… I can believe he was dirty. What I can't believe is that he was the one who killed your family. All these years we've worked with him and he knew what he'd done." Devon slapped the tray sitting over his bed. "I knew we had a rat, but the rest of this is hitting me like a brick."

Jackson stared out the window at the cars below. He was glad the nightmare was over. No one could be as blindsided as he was.

Devon's tone lightened. "What will happen with Allison?"

"What do you mean? She's going back to Houston."

"Is that what you want?"

Jackson didn't know how to answer that question.

It was one thing to think something in his head, but it was another to admit it out loud.

"I care about her. It's just, well, you know."

"It's okay, Jackson. You'll know when it's right. But you've got to stop living in the past. Life is too short. Matter of fact, this has changed me. I took things for granted a lot. But not anymore. I have a whole new appreciation for getting out of the bed in the morning. So, is that what you want?"

It hurt to hear his friend talk about his own death. "What? For her to go back to Houston? No, it's not what I want, but life doesn't always give us what we want." He stopped talking to swallow the lump in his throat.

Allison walked into the hospital room with Karen to find Jackson and Devon in a somber mood. Her heart skidded to a halt. She prayed nothing else bad had happened.

"Did you boys lose your dog?" Karen sat two cups of coffee on the table.

Jackson grinned. "We need to get out of here and let this man rest so he can get back home." He gave Devon a pat on the shoulder and hugged Karen.

"It was nice meeting you, Karen." Allison turned to Devon. "I'm so glad you're going to be okay. I'll keep you in my prayers."

Devon nodded. "Thank you. Looking forward to seeing you again, Allison."

Jackson led the way to the elevators without saying a word. His quiet demeanor was a lot like when they'd first met. She'd hoped after all they'd been through that he'd open up to her more. But reading his moods hadn't gotten any easier. Matter of fact, it only seemed to be getting harder.

Once they climbed into his truck, he turned to face her. "Are you ready to go to your sister's house?"

"Sure. I lost my phone, so I can't call them."

Jackson sat staring out the front window. He was too quiet. Something was on his mind. She wished he would spit it out and get it over with.

"Okay." He turned the ignition on but didn't back out.

Allison's nerves were on edge. She didn't dare push him into talking right now. He'd been through as much as she had. If she was going to compare their experiences, it was safe to say he'd been through more. She knew it was hard for him to process everything. It only seemed fair to give him the time and space he needed.

Jackson pulled out of the parking space and headed for Maddie's house. Allison watched him as he drove. His rugged features looked tired and haggard, but it didn't take away from his handsome looks. There was no denying her feelings for him. But would he ever be able to move on? She didn't expect him to forget about his family, but could he ever love again? She wondered if he knew how much God wanted him to be happy.

Allison longed to tell him how much she cared for him, but she couldn't be sure of how he felt. She wondered if those moments they'd shared were because of their life-or-death situation. She'd learned a lot about him since they'd met. He didn't pretend to care if he didn't. Jackson Archer wasn't the kind of man who got close to someone because of circumstances. He did it because he wanted to.

Going back to Houston wasn't something she was

happy about now. Life without him seemed wrong. After all they'd been through, saying goodbye would be the hardest thing she'd ever done. But would telling him how she felt push him away?

They turned onto Maddie's street, and the knot in her stomach tightened. The quiet ride had been torture. She'd never seen him so deep in thought and she couldn't take it anymore.

"Jackson, what's wrong?"

He smiled at her. "Nothing. I'm fine."

She wasn't buying it. "No, you're not. Would you like to talk?"

The words had hardly left her mouth and already she regretted them. She braced herself for what he was about to say. He pulled in to Maddie's driveway. Allison reached for the door handle as soon as Jackson parked the truck.

"Wait."

Her heart pounded in her chest. She stopped with her hand still on the handle. After a few uncomfortable seconds he finally broke his silence.

"I want to talk, Allison."

She let go of the door and faced him. Her heart pounded her chest. "Sure."

"I didn't think I would ever find out who killed my wife and daughter. And my unborn son."

She gasped at his shocking words. Allison had no idea his wife had been pregnant. Why was he telling her this now?

"Jackson, I didn't know. I'm sorry." Tears sprang to her eyes and fell to her cheeks before she could make them stop.

"It didn't seem like something I needed to bring up. But I wanted you to know."

"I'm so sorry for everything you went through, Jackson."

"I can tell. A lot of people say it, but you actually mean it. I've always seen that in you. You're not like most women. You are the most patient woman I've ever met, other than my mother."

Allison laughed. His mother was a great lady and she hoped someday she'd get to see her again. But that all depended on what Jackson was about to tell her. She could see the anguish in his face. This was hard for him. Not that it was any easier for her, but she was much better at expressing her feelings. If this thing between them was going to go anywhere, she would have to be the one to start. She took a deep breath and began to speak when he cut her off.

"How's your knee?"

"What?"

He pointed at her leg. "Your stitches."

She waved a hand. "It's fine." If she was going to do this, she needed to get it over with. She inhaled a sharp breath. "Jackson Archer, I fell in love with you. From your dry sense of humor and your mood swings, right down to your grumpy attitude. You not only protected me out there, but you risked your life trying to save mine."

"Allison, it's my job."

"I know. Don't misunderstand me. This isn't about some infatuation. I'm old enough to know the difference. It's not that. I can't explain what I feel. I only know that it's real."

Shock registered on his face, and she braced for his reply.

"It's my job. And even if it wasn't, I would've done the same thing."

"Maybe it is your job, but you didn't have to try to do it single-handed. You could've turned me over to the feds from the beginning."

"Schmille would've let the cartel kill you."

Allison didn't know why she was arguing with him about this. It was more than obvious he was ignoring what she'd confessed to him. "What are we doing, Jackson?"

His green eyes darkened. "Come over here." He reached out and pulled her to him.

His hand slipped through her hair to caress the back of her neck. He leaned in and kissed her mouth with a tenderness she'd never experienced before. Allison touched his face with her palm. The pressure on her lips grew more intense as he kissed her. If she didn't know better, he was kissing her like their lives depended on it. And in a way, they did.

He pulled back and gazed into her eyes. "I can't lose anything else in my life. I've already lost everything once. I don't know if I can do that again. Right now, I don't even know if I would want kids again." He raked a hand into his hair. "There's so many complications to this."

"Jackson, I think you're getting a little ahead of yourself. I have faith that this will work out. In fact, I have a Bible verse that hangs in my office. It's from Proverbs 20:24. 'Since the Lord is directing our steps, why try to understand everything that happens along the way?'

Every time I get scared or worried, I always think about that verse. I put my faith in Him and I keep going."

"You'll need to have enough faith for the both of us. I had a relationship with God once. I turned my back when my family was taken. I wish I hadn't. I spent years wallowing in misery. Going through all this with you changed me. I found myself praying for you, talking to Him. I realized it wasn't God who left me. I was the one who left Him." He kissed her forehead. "I'm scared, Allison."

Her eyes widened. "You take on drug dealers, the cartel and people with guns pointed at your head, but I scare you?"

He laughed and tapped the end of her nose. "To death."

She giggled at the serious expression on his face.

His hand cupped her cheek. "I can't let you go, Allison. Somehow, when I least expected it, I fell in love with you. And before we go any further here, I need to make sure you know one thing."

She held her breath, waiting for him to finish.

"No one can ever take Hope's place."

"Jackson, that's not what I—"

"Let me finish. That's not what I'm looking for. It's never been what I wanted. I knew if I ever loved again, it wouldn't be to replace her. I love you for who you are. Allison Moore, I may have saved your life, but make no mistake, you were sent to save mine. I love you, Allison."

Jackson kissed her lips. He pulled away, and she took a deep breath to steady her heart. She narrowed her eyes at him. "I love you, too, Jackson. But do you think you can tone down that salty attitude a little bit?"

His laughter filled the cab of the truck. "Oh, I think I can do anything for you. Now, let's go tell your sister I'm taking you back to Houston." He kissed her forehead. "And I'm not letting you out of my sight for the rest of your life."

Allison kissed his cheek. "That sounds like the best plan I've ever heard."

EPILOGUE

One and a half years later

Allison raced to the front door. "They're here!"

Jackson watched as she turned to grin at him. It still amazed him how much his life had changed in such a short time. That cold night on the highway now seemed like ages ago. Allison had found him at a time when he doubted God had anything good left to give him. How wrong he'd been.

He watched her as she made her way to the foyer. Memories of their wedding day flashed before him and brought a smile to his lips. He would never forget how beautiful she looked. A few months after the wedding they'd moved to Houston, and a short year later they'd been blessed with a son. Life couldn't be better.

"I'm so glad they're here!" She smoothed her hair and clothes.

"Let them in." He laughed at her childlike excitement.

Allison opened the door to Maddie and her family. She hugged each of them and kissed the girls.

"Where is he? Where's baby Aaron, Aunt Ally?"

Phoebe bounced up and down as she pulled on Allison's shirt.

"He's sleeping right now, but as soon as he wakes up, you can give him lots of hugs and kisses."

Jackson walked toward the door. Charlotte toddled up to him and held up her arms. He picked her up and kissed her cheek. "I've got barbecue on the pit and the football game on in the den. Scott, want to watch the game?"

"Oh! That reminds me. I have cookies in the oven." Allison tapped the end of Phoebe's nose. "Chocolate chip. Your favorite."

The sound of crying echoed from the hallway. Maddie piped up. "I'll get the baby."

Allison hugged her sister. "Thank you. I'll get dinner ready. Phoebe, go help your mom. Jackson, can you help me in the kitchen for a second?"

Jackson handed Charlotte off to Scott. "Sure."

Once inside the kitchen, Allison turned to him and smiled.

"What do you need help with?" He grabbed for a cookie lying on a plate by the oven.

She tapped his hand. Her tone turned serious. "Put that down. I have something to tell you."

"What's wrong?" He dropped the cookie and gave her his full attention.

"Avery Guerrero called me about ten minutes ago. He said he is looking to expand his hotels into the Austin area. He said if I'm interested, he could relocate me to Stonewater. That's if you want to move back."

Jackson looked into her eyes. This woman had given him so much, and she was still willing to make sacrifices for him.

"Allison, I like it here. I enjoy working with the Harris County Sheriff's Department. I like our house, our church. I love our life here. I want to raise our son here. Do you really want to move?"

Her eyes drifted to the floor. "I don't know. I just thought..."

Jackson's heart melted. "You thought what? That my old life was in Stonewater and that I missed it?" He pulled her to him and held her against his chest. "Allison, you are my life. You and Aaron are my world. You've made me happier than I ever thought I could be. You taught me that God does heal, and that He never leaves me. My life was in Stonewater once, but it's here with you now. So stop worrying about me."

Allison giggled and pulled away enough to look up at him. She stood on her tiptoes and kissed his lips. "Always salty. I love you, Jackson."

Jackson's laugh filled the kitchen. "I love you, Allison."

* * * * *

Dear Reader,

How great is it that we serve a God of second chances? One who knows us better than we know ourselves. No matter how hard we try to make things happen in our own way, or in our own time, it won't work if it's not God's plan for our lives.

In this story, Jackson is a man scarred by pain and loss. He never considers God's plan for his happiness until Allison is thrown into his life. Her faith, even in the most trying circumstances, makes Jackson reconsider the distance he's put between himself and God.

After writing for more than twenty years, I wondered when my time would come to be a published author. I was busy as a wife, mom and full-time elementary school teacher. Now that my kids are grown, I look back and wonder how I could've fit another career into my life. Just as in Jackson and Allison's story, God's timing has always been perfect in my life, too. *Accidental Target* is my debut novel for Love Inspired Suspense.

Thank you for reading *Accidental Target*. I hope you enjoyed reading it as much as I enjoyed writing it.

God's blessings,
Theresa

**WE HOPE YOU ENJOYED
THIS BOOK FROM**

LOVE INSPIRED SUSPENSE
INSPIRATIONAL ROMANCE

Courage. Danger. Faith.

Find strength and determination in stories
of faith and love in the face of danger.

6 NEW BOOKS AVAILABLE EVERY MONTH!

A K-9 officer and a forensics specialist must work together to solve a murder and stay alive.

Read on for a sneak preview of
Scene of the Crime *by Sharon Dunn,*
the next book in the True Blue K-9 Unit: Brooklyn series
available September 2020 from Love Inspired Suspense.

Brooklyn K-9 Unit Officer Jackson Davison caught movement out of the corner of his eye: a face in the trees fading out of view. His heart beat a little faster. Was someone watching him? The hairs on the back of Jackson's neck stood at attention as a light breeze brushed his face. Even as he studied the foliage, he felt the weight of a gaze on him. The sound of Smokey's barking brought his mission back into focus.

When he caught up with his partner, the dog was sitting. The signal that he'd found something. "Good boy." Jackson tossed out the toy he carried on his belt for Smokey to play with, his reward for doing his job. The dog whipped the toy back and forth in his mouth.

"Drop," Jackson said. He picked up the toy and patted Smokey on the head. "Sit. Stay."

The body, partially covered by branches, was clothed in neutral colors and would not be easy to spot unless you were looking for it.

He keyed his radio. "Officer Davison here. I've got a body in Prospect Park. Male Caucasian under the age of forty, about two hundred yards in, just southwest of the Brooklyn Botanic Garden."

Dispatch responded, "Ten-four. Help is on the way."

He studied the trees just in time to catch the face again, barely visible, like a fading mist. He was being watched. "Did you see something?" Jackson shouted. "Did you call this in?"

The person turned and ran, disappearing into the thick brush.

Jackson took off in the direction the runner had gone. As his feet pounded the hard earth, another thought occurred to him. Was this the person who had shot the man in the chest? Sometimes criminals hung around to witness the police response to their handiwork.

His attention was drawn to a garbage can just as an object hit the back of his head with intense force. Pain radiated from the base of his skull. He crumpled to the ground and his world went black.

Don't miss
Scene of the Crime *by Sharon Dunn,*
available wherever Love Inspired Suspense books
and ebooks are sold.

LoveInspired.com

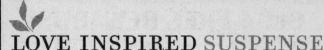